The Geek Girl

And the Quarterback

James J. Caterino

Other published works by James J. Caterino include:
Pop Songs or Poetry
Ready, Set, Action
Time Travel Stories
The Promise
Pop Star
The Quarterback
Miami Noir 1987
The Girl from the Stars
The Last Neanderthal
Watch the Skies

Chapter 1 – Summer of 1987

Delila Frank sat still in her usual aisle seat, listening to the beautiful music, reading every last credit, as she always did.

When the projector finally stopped and the house lights came on, she took out her over-saturated handkerchief, slipped her glasses off, and dabbed away the last evidence of her tears before leaving her seat and exiting the theater as the between showings clean-up crew of teen workers came in and did their thing.

As was often the case, Delila was alone.

She had just seen *Harry and the Hendersons* on its opening night and the sweetness of the film had really touched her. She could not wait to write a review for the school paper, if Miss Allen came through with getting approval to publish a special summer edition of the Coral Springs Colt Gazette, her high school newspaper.

She took out the small pad and pen that she carried and began to think of a few key thoughts to jot down as she left the AMC theater and headed up the escalator to Dan Marino's Sports Bar and Restaurant, where she would be meeting her Aunt Valerie, whom she called Aunt Val, and her aunt's boyfriend Scott.

It was Friday June 5th, 1987, the first day of the summer vacation before her senior year of at Coral Springs High School in South Florida. But for a big chunk of this summer, at least during the week, Delila would be staying fifty miles south of her home in Coral Springs, down here in the heart of Miami with her Aunt Val in Coconut Grove.

It was an effective way to avoid the brutal commute up and down I-95 each day to her much coveted summer job, an internship at the Miami Herald. Plus, it was a chance to get a break from her increasingly nagging parents and the little brother Jeff, whom they kept holding up as the "well-rounded" role model Delila should seek to emulate.

The internship at the Herald was a paying job and would be a major feather on her resume for her college application to the only school she was interested in, the University of Miami, where she would have dual major in film and writing to help launch her career as a film critic.

She had it all figured out.

Despite her organized sense of purpose, not to mention her good grades, Delila had been getting grief from her parents. Just before her departure for Miami last night, they summoned her for a meeting to express their concerns about her lack of a social life.

“Honey, I’m worried about you,” her mother said. “You know, this is your senior year.”

“Yeah Mom, I’m aware of that,” Delila said.

“Maybe use this time down there with Valerie to get out and meet some people,” her mother added. “Sometimes my sister is a bit too…aggressive in her lifestyle. But she knows everyone in that city and I’m sure she knows all the places the young people hang out.”

“Mom, really?” Delila said.

“You just need some friends,” her father chipped in,

“I have friends Dad,” Delila protested. “Linda and Spaz are my friends.”

“I mean, like normal friends,” he quipped.

True, Linda and Spaz were eccentric. But they really were two people she could count on. The only two.

“And at least Linda and Roger are in the band,” her mom said, referring to Spaz by his real name.

“That’s what you need too,” her mom said.

“I think they require you to actually play an instrument to join that particular organization Mom,” Delila said.

“No silly,” she said. “I just mean maybe you need to join some group where you interact with others.”

Uggg.

A week earlier, even her guidance counselor at school used the opportunity of a meeting about college applications to beat her up about her lack of friends.

"I always see you eating lunch alone and reading a book," he said. "Reading is good. But you need balance. Maybe when you get back for your senior year, forgo the book at lunch and start mingling a bit. Colleges like students who have demonstrated strong social skills. You don't belong to any school organizations or participate in any functions."

"I write for the school newspaper," she shot back.

"Yes, I see that," he said, looking over her file. "But you just write movie reviews. You go sit alone in the dark and watch a movie. And write about it. Nothing social about that Miss Frank."

Delila had to use all her restraint not to curse at him. Or throw something at him.

She did all that was asked of her. Had perfect grades. Never got in trouble. Like ever in her life. Never bothered anyone. So why was she getting so much shit?

She had it all figured out, she reminded herself gain.

She loved movies. And she hated humans.

Her experience with people throughout most of her seventeen years had been unpleasant at best. Friends was the last thing she needed. She had her movies. She had her writing. She was good to go.

Or so she thought.

Valerie and Scott were waiting for inside Dan Marino's at a corner booth.

She gave her Aunt Val a hug and said a cordial hello to Scott.

Scott was new on the scene, but Delila could already tell he was an ass. Just like all of Aunt Val's boyfriends. On more than one occasion, she had caught him leeringly looking her up and down like a piece of meat. He was dating the hottest catch in Miami and yet still could not control himself from salivating over her underage niece. And the thing was, he wasn't even good-looking.

Yet, like all the previous losers, somehow her aunt saw something in him.

Her Aunt Val was a successful, bordering on famous, photographer, and she was a stunningly beautiful woman. But her taste in men was downright awful. Even her parents agreed with her on that one.

Despite Scott's presence, it was a nice dinner. The service was good and the food much better that you would think for a celebrity themed sports bar. Delila told them about the movie and then Val, who had pulled some strings to get her the gig at The Herald, told her what to expect when she began the internship tomorrow, on Saturday morning at nine AM sharp.

Walking out of Dan Marino's, Delila was fully expecting to call it a night and head back to Val's place, but as they walked past a karaoke bar, both her aunt and Scott insisted that they go inside.

The strains of someone attempting to sing Tony Orlando and Dawn's "Tie a Yellow Ribbon" emanated out from the bar into the plaza. Attempting to sing being the key phrase here.

"Are you kidding me Aunt Val?" Delila tried to protest as Val and Scott waved her on to follow them inside.

It was useless to resist. She had taken the bus down here for the movie and did not feel like walking the two miles or so back up into the North Grove where Val lived. Thus, she followed her aunt and Scott into the cacophony of chaos.

Delila stepped inside and experienced a complete sensory overload.

The neon lights, the rowdy crowd, a mix of drunken yuppies still in their work attire and young adults and college kids; really pretty girls in really short skirts and guys in extra tight t-shirts that looked about two sized too small.

In the left corner of bar, right up against the stage, a particularly rowdy group of guys caught her attention. Not so much because they were boisterous, but because they were so freaking huge.

Scott tapped on her shoulder and pointed at them.

"Canes players!" he said.

That explained why they were such large humans.

Around these parts, the University of Miami football team had become legendary. But as she scanned over the group more closely, she realized one of them was not a Miami Hurricane, nor a college student at all. Indeed, Delila recognized him because he was a high school student.

His name was Rick Strasser, the quarterback of her very own Coral Springs High School Colts, and a local legend in his own right. Even Scott recognized him.

"Isn't that your quarterback?" Scott said. "What's he doing here hanging with the Canes? I thought he was committed to Notre Dame because of his old man. Buy hey, if we can snag him, that would be fucking huge."

Scott was right.

Delila was no sports junkie. But it was impossible to exist in Coral Springs and not know that Rick Strasser was the most sought-after high school quarterback in the country and was fully expected to follow in his father's footsteps and go to Notre Dame on the way to an illustrious career in the NFL.

And yet, here he was, hanging with the Miami players as if his future lay up the road at the University of Miami in Coral Gables, rather than out in the heartland of America near the golden dome.

Then, Rick Strasser did something even more shocking and out of character, at least based on his public persona, since Delila had never stood anywhere in the vicinity of Rick Strasser, let alone actually talked to him.

Egged on by his Miami Hurricane buddies, Rick Strasser leapt up onto the stage and took the microphone.

As he stared at the monitor and waited for the music to start and the lyrics to scroll, the house lights shifted around, and for a brief moment there was a spotlight, beaming down right on top of Delila.

Rick Strasser looked right at her.

They locked eyes.

She was mortified.

The spotlight moved over to him, and the music began.

The song was "Can't Take My Eyes Off of You" by Frankie Valli and The Four Seasons. Strasser started to sing, and two more shocking surprises hit Delila with a wallop.

One, Brock Strasser could sing. He could really sing, and as the song continued to build into the explosive chorus, his voice and performance kept getting better.

Two, as he dug into the song more and more, he was looking right at Delila. So much so, it caught the attention of the Miami Hurricane football players and other patrons in the bar, including Val and Scott.

What the hell is happening?

Delila wanted to die on the spot, and as her heart pounded and her chest tightened, she thought she might just do that.

Rick Strasser was singing to her, and the entire place was looking at her. She feared she would pass out any second and the embarrassment of the event would haunt her the rest of her life.

Somehow, she managed to stay conscious and erect during it all and as the song ended to a thunderous ovation, she fought to catch her breath as she ducked down and tried to head for the exit.

She was intercepted by her Aunt Val.

"You just been called out. Or hit on. Or both," Val said.

"Now it's your time girl. Time to shine," Val added. "Get up there and answer. I know you can sing Dee, because I heard you do it many times when you were young."

"That was a long time ago," Delila said. "And trust me when I tell you that guy has no idea who I am. And he's taken. You know, the head cheerleader homecoming mean-girl type. The type that could turn my senior year into a real-life horror film."

"Hey, I'm not talking about marriage or even dating here. I'm taking about having fun. Something you need. Just sing back at him. Come on Dee. I know for a fact they have *Take My Breath Away* available up there, perfect for your voice," Val said. "You can do this girl."

"I…I can't," Delila said. "I'm sorry."

It was all too much. She panicked.

She quickly stepped around Val and scurried out the front door and escaped into the safety of the outside plaza.

The next day, Saturday, her first official day at the Miami Herald, was more or less an orientation.

She met everyone, and most importantly, she met all the entertainment writers, including her role model, the Herald's much respected film critic Bill Cosford.

Even though her true duties would amount to being little more than a coffee-fetching gopher, just being around this place gave her a jolt of energy. There was a lot to take in and all of it was a welcome distraction. A distraction from her obsessive thoughts about last night and the star quarterback who was singing to her.

She began to see Rick Strasser as a real person now, not just some distant, mythic local celebrity jock who just happened to attend the same high school as her.

And then there was that way he looked at her. The way he sang to her. He really did sing to her. It made her think of things. Of far-fetched possibilities she never would have imagined or dreamt of in a million years.

But she knew she had to put those thoughts out of her head. He was probably buzzed, caught up in the moment of the party atmosphere, and had mistaken her in the darkness of the bar for some local chickita tourist hottie.

Plus, there was another reason why Delila had to forget all about last night.

The head cheerleader girlfriend she had mentioned to Val.

Her name was Heather and she had a well-earned reputation for being a first class bullying bitch. Delila had a past experience with her type back up Pennsylvania, before her parents had moved them down here to South Florida.

It happened when during Junior High and for an eternal two years, her life became a living hell. An influential social queen and her robots decided, whether out of jealousy or some perceived nonexistent threat, to destroy her and they did so with extreme prejudice. It changed Delila. She went from being an outgoing, socially active, vibrant young adolescent, to being a reclusive loner wary of human contact.

On the way to school, between classes, lunchtime, gym, and walking home; back in junior high she had lived her life in a constant state fear. To an adult or to anyone who never experienced being targeted by a group of unrelenting bullies, it would sound all so trivial. But to the victim, it is horrific. Living under that day-to-day stress was unbearable. Delila never, ever, wanted to go through that again. And that is exactly the kind of trouble that was waiting for her if she put herself out there and risked incurring the wrath of the ruling class of the school.

That is why she must erase everything about last night and Rick Strasser at the karaoke bar from her mind.

But try as she might, she just could not stop thinking about the celebrity quarterback, and the way he had looked at her.

Rick woke up in Jamal's dorm room with a clear head, thankful that despite drinking and being buzzed last night, he felt pretty good. Not so for Jamal he thought when he heard the painful moans from across the room as his friend dragged himself out of the bed.

Jamal was his longtime friend and a former teammate at Coral Springs High School. Jamal was now a Miami Hurricane and doing his best to make sure Rick would soon be the same. It would be the easiest sales job in the world, because unknown to his father who bled Notre Dame gold, Rick had dreamed of playing for the Hurricanes since he was thirteen years old.

Jamal was staying on campus during the summer break between his freshman and sophomore years to take some classes and train at the facilities. Officially, Rick was just here to visit a friend. But in reality, and as far as the Miami coaches were concerned, this was a visit and Rick was their guy.

Rick had no idea why he was so fearful to just come out and tell his dad the truth.

Maybe it was because of all the schools his son wanted to go to instead of Notre Dame, it was their hated nemesis in the already infamous so called "Catholics vs. Convicts" rivalry. It wasn't so much that he worried about his father reacting in anger, but that he feared breaking the heart of his number one supporter.

So, for now, Rick just continued avoiding the confrontation, or as a knowing internal voice said to him, taking the coward's way out.

But none of that was really on his mind this morning. His thoughts were about last night, and that alluring, mysterious, and yet oh so familiar girl who had caught his eye at the karaoke bar. It had been hard to take in the details and get a good look at her with the stage lights glaring into his eyes. The fact that he had been drinking did not help either. But that mystery only added to her seductive appeal. There had just been something about her.

Was she a tourist or a local?

Maybe even a student at Miami?

And that vibe she gave off. The cute shape. In between the glares of the stage lights, he did notice that. And the curly black hair, the glasses, the red lips. So geek, yet so chic. A librarian concealing another persona underneath. Like she was hiding something. He craved more.

Rick had a longtime girlfriend named Heather, at this point he was with her more out of habit than any real passion. But he was as loyal as they came. So, he knew nothing could really happen here. This was his imagination running away. A wishful fantasy.

But still…

He could not stop thinking about this mystery girl.

Rick spent Saturday morning working out with Jamal at the Canes' facility, then hitting the weight room followed by some seven-on-seven drills with a group of Miami players. He even got to meet with and throw to Michael Irvin, the Junior superstar wide receiver, who like Rick, was a sought after local high school recruit when he had played for St. Thoman Aquinas in Plantation.

When Rick took over the Coral Springs Colts' starting quarterback as a sophomore, Jamal was a Parade All-American senior coveted by a slew of Division I schools. The two of them became roommates at camp and instantly developed a chemistry on the field, where Rick threw fifteen touchdown passes to him, and off the field, where they became best friends.

Even here, going up against Miami's elite defensive backs and linebackers, Rick was able to thread the needle and get the ball to Jamal again and again. The drills were going well. Too well. A small crowd of onlookers had noticed the razor-sharp passes and recognized the quarterback who was throwing them.

Including someone taking pictures and jotting down notes. A reporter.

"Don't sweat it brother," Jamal said. "That's not The Herald. Just someone from the school paper. It's not an official workout. No coaches. And no real media."

"Okay, cool," Rick said trying to play it off. But a pit of anxiety remained in his stomach. Things had a way of getting out. The South Florida football community was an interconnected place. And if his dad found out what he was really doing this weekend…well, it just was something he didn't want to deal with right now.

Later that day, after he showered, Rick had lunch with Jamal in the cafeteria. Then hopped into his metallic blue Dodge Charger to make the drive back up to Coral Springs and forgot all about the reporter.

But the karaoke bar geek girl, she was more on his mind than ever. He spent the entire drive up I-95 daydreaming about her, imagining what she might be like. What they might be like, together.

Chapter 2 – First Day of School

Delila's social anxiety kicked into high gear the second she stepped outside her mother's car and began making her way up the sidewalk and into the moving mass of rambunctious students.

The culture shock of the first day back to school was always brutal for her, especially after the pleasant and productive summer she had in Miami, staying with her Aunt Val, working at the Herald, and going to lots and lots of movies.

She spotted Suzy and Spaz, enthusiastically weaving through the crowd toward her. They were a sight for sore eyes. She felt her anxiety levels begin to come down.

Six feet plus with a waifish, spidery frame, Spaz was a walking sports encyclopedia with a thing for statistics. Delilia was sure he could recite all of Rick Strasser's, or any one else's, passing statistics from memory. Suzy was a cheerful redhead whose standard attire was jeans, a flannel shirt unbuttoned to expose a Van Halen t-shirt, and a pair of canvas sneakers. Both shared Delila's passion for cinema, and like her, neither had any friends, except for each other.

"Welcome Coconut Grove Girl," Suzy said, giving her a hug.

"Yeah, how was Miami?" Spaz asked.

"And working at the Herald?" Suzy asked.

"Did you get to meet Bill Cosford?" Spaz asked.

"Oh that's right Dee! What's he like?" Suzy said.

"Miami was awesome. My Aunt Val was cool. Working at the Herald, eh, mostly fetching coffee and picking up laundry," Delila said. "And yes, I did indeed get to meet the man and pick his brain a bit. He's very nice. Really laid back."

"Cool!" they both said in unison.

"But most important of all, there is one thing I'm dying to know right now," Spaz said.

Delila felt a jolt of panic hit her.

Did Spaz somehow know about her encounter Rick Strasser at the karaoke bar? Spaz seemed to know everything about everyone, and she was sure he had his ear tuned to the gossip and chatter of the South Florida jock culture given his thing for sports and stats. If word got back to Strasser's queen bitch girlfriend Heather, Delila's senior year would turn into a Brian De Palma horror film, except she would be a Carrie without the telekinetic powers to defend herself.

"What's that?" Delila asked, holding her breath as she awaited his response.

"Oh my God, the color on your face just drained," Suzy noted.

"Relax Dee. It's nothing bad, I promise," Spaz said. "I'm just dying to know your top movie pick of the summer."

"Oh that," Delila said, breathing in a sigh of relief.

"Well Spaz, you're just going to have to wait for Friday's issue of The Coral Springs Colt Gazette."

"You know my rule," Delila added.

"No spoilers!" the three of them said in unison.

"Tease," Spaz said.

Somehow Delila made it through the first day of her senior year and headed downstairs to the basement floor for the eighth and final period of the day where she would spend her study hall in the newspaper room. She wanted to turn in her "A Summer at the Movies" article, a feature piece for the special premiere edition of the paper to launch the new school year.

She sat and waited as Miss Allen, the faculty editor and chief, read the article.

"Insightful and smoothly written," Miss Allen said approvingly. "And that top ten best summer movies of 1987 list…*The Untouchables*, oh I agree…*Robocop*, a little dark and subversive for my tastes but bold and smart…*Full Metal Jacket*, hey it's Stanley Kubrick…*No Way Out*, Kevin Costner had a great summer! *Dirty Dancing*, sleeper yes! *The Lost Boys*, still need to see but looked like good, scary fun. *Innerspace*, it was a joy. I loved it. *Harry and the Hendersons*, looked cute, so I'll check it out on home video for my niece and nephew based on your recommendation. *Adventures in Babysitting*. The coolest poster. And rounding out your summer top ten is *Can't Buy Me Love*. Oh my, you are a secret romantic."

Delila felt herself blush.

"Wonderful work as always Delila," Miss Allen said. "We'll give you a lead in on the front page."

Miss Allen smiled, but Delila could tell something else was on her mind.

"And now, I have something new for you," she said. "Something really special. Something that will help make your application for the University of Miami film school a shoe-in."

"Umm…wow," Delila was taken aback, and very intrigued. "Okay, you have my attention,"

"Follow me," Miss Allen said, leading her back into the storage room.

She pulled out an oversized metal case, set it down on a table, and dramatically opened it with a "Behold!"

Delila recognized it immediately.

"That's the new Sony video camera, the format with the micro-cassettes , eight millimeter tape," Delila said.

"Yep," Miss Allen said. "And this fine piece of brand new hardware is now the official property of the Coral Springs Colt Gazette."

"We have a budget to be able to buy something like this?" Delila asked.

"Hell no. We're lucky we get the district to spring enough to pay the printer for our run each Friday," Miss Allen said. "This sweet camera was donated to us by the good people at Channel Sixteen, the PBS station. Along with a budget of one thousand dollars."

"A thousand dollars? A budget? For what?" Delila asked.

"To make a movie," Miss Allen said. "Specifically, a documentary that they will be screening on air this November as part of a local film festival of sorts. Nine other schools were chosen to participate. November does not give us much time, so you'll have to move on this fast. We can use the budget for expenses, or to hire an editor, rent time on the Avid machine they use at the station, and take care of the music. Either hire a composer or get rights to some songs. Or you can leave it unscored. That'll all be up to you. Creative choices. That's what it's all about."

For the first time in a long time, Delila felt really excited about being here at school. Even inspired.

"Wow Miss Allen. This is amazing!" she said.

"Yes. Amazing and right up your alley given your movie obsession and film school future. And this project will go along way to make that future happen," Miss Allen said.

"I'm just…beside myself," Delila said. "I don't know what to say other than thank you."

"Say that you are going to make a kick ass documentary and blow away those other nine schools and bring us the top prize in that festival," Miss Allen said.

"Yes. Of course. All that," Delila said. "I won't let you down Miss Allen."

"I know you won't Dee," Miss Allen said.

"And I'll start brainstorming some ideas right away and begin story boarding," Delila said. "As soon as I can come with the right focus for this film, with your approval of course."

Miss Allen grew quiet and gave her a bit of a serious look.

"I'm afraid that's already been decided," she said.

"Oh? You already have a topic in mind?" Delila asked.

"No, not me Dee. The station," Miss Allen said. "This camera, and that budget…they come with strings attached."

"I understand," Delila said. "A director for hire. I can certainly handle that for my first gig behind the camera. Plenty of time to be an auteur down the road. Right?"

"Exactly!" Miss Allen said. "Remember Spielberg got his start directing television episodes for Universal."

Delila nodded, thinking about his segment of *Night Gallery.*

The thought excited Delila. Maybe her future lay in making movies rather than just writing about them. Either way, she would be happy.

"Anyway," Delila said. "What subject does the station want us to cover?"

"More of a person than a subject," Miss Allen said.

"Oh?" Delila said.

"They want a behind the scenes look at Coral Springs High's most famous resident," Miss Allen said.

Delila felt an overwhelming sense of nervous dread. She feared she might pass out from an anxiety overload because she knew exactly what Miss Allen was going to say next.

"Rick Strasser."

Chapter 3 – What I Really Want is to Direct

Delila's parents were thrilled when she told them about her film project. Mainly because it would, as her mother put it, "force her to engage with others".

Her father's eyes lit up at the mention of Rick Strasser. Like everyone else in the community, he was enamored with the quarterback's talent and mystique. He seemed more interested in obtaining an autograph than he was in what a potential asset this project might be for her career in film. Her little brother Jeff kept bringing her things that he wanted her to try and get Rick to sign. Quarterbacks were the new rockstars, especially here in the football-centric community of South Florida, Dan Marino, and the Miami Dolphins.

The next morning during their traditional gathering before home room, she broke the news to Suzy and Spaz.

Suzy was sincerely excited for her.

Delila wished she could tell her friend the entire backstory and share the secret karaoke bar encounter she had with Rick Strasser over the summer. But she knew it was secret she had to keep for now. Especially in front of Spaz. He was sweet and a true friend. But he had loose lips.

Of course, Spaz was euphoric to hear about her documentary assignment and began rattling off Strasser's passing statistics. And he had some breaking news of his own.

"Oh my God, given the break-up, this is perfect timing! The movie Gods have smiled upon you Dee," Spaz said.

"What? Why?" Delila asked.

"The epic breakup of course," Spaz said.

"What break up?" Suzy asked.

"You guys didn't here? You two really do need to get out more," Spaz said. "They broke up."

"Who?" Delila asked.

"The subject of your soon to be cinematic masterpiece and the bitchy Goddess with the oh so perfect body he's been dating for the past six months. Tanta Gusto tongue-able Heather. I mean, I heard that's what they call her."

"Dude, stop," Suzy said. "But really? Rick Strasser and Heather head cheerleader broke up."

"It's a fact," Spaz said. "And she dumped him."

"Damn!" Suzy said.

"Hey Dee, you okay? You look kinda pale," Spaz said. "You want this film to be a classy piece. So, if I were you, I'd steer clear of any gossipy dating questions."

"I plan to," Delila said. "Steer clear that is."

Delila felt a whole new wave of nervous panic flood over her.

Approaching Rick Strasser to do this film was something she had already been dreading. And now, a complicated situation had somehow just become even more awkward and messy.

The bell sounded indicating the start of the school day. She took a deep breath, headed into homeroom, and began to strategize about when and how she was going the approach the subject of her film.

Rick's senior year began with the two things he did his best to avoid in his personal life. Confrontation and drama. Both came to him courtesy of Heather McGear, his now ex-girlfriend.

She ended their relationship with the same cold precision with which she had started it.

Some six months ago she had decided that Rick was to be her boyfriend and he certainly was not going to put up any resistance. After all, she was unquestionably beautiful, extremely sexy in an instantly arousing way, and very convincing.

And very physical.

Heather was not technically the first girl he had been with. There had been an awkward, very clumsy encounter with an older girl in his neighborhood a few years back that was best forgotten. But Heather was the first time he had fully functional sex, and she was very passionate. But she was also very possessive. So much so, that Rick began to fear for any poor girl who might glance in his direction when she was around. Her nickname of "Queen Bitch" was well earned. Of course, it was a nickname nobody dared speak out loud in her formidable presence.

The physical part of their relationship, that worked for sure. But once the initial fire of that died down, he realized how little they had in common.

Rick had three passions. Football, music, and movies.

Despite being the head cheerleader, Heather had no real actual interest in football. Anytime he tried to talk about practice or a game or a college trying to recruit him, she'd look away as if bored or she'd outright cut him off. She mocked him for learning to play the guitar and keyboard. And he had to drag her kicking and screaming to the movies because she was afraid of missing out on some party somewhere where she could showcase her exquisitely pampered form in the latest designer fashions.

After a while, Rick just felt trapped.

So, when Heather greeted him the first day of school by terminating their relationship with extreme prejudice so she could "grow as a person" before college, he was shocked. He felt some hurt, had a bit of a bruised ego, but more than anything else, he just felt relieved.

Sure, there was some sadness with that hurt. After all, they had been together for six months. But he would deal with that by focusing all his thoughts and energy on this week's season opener, an away game at Ely, their non-conference archrival and one of the best teams in all of South Florida.

Rick went through the morning feeling a bit lost. This was the first full day after the break-up and it felt odd not be meeting up with Heather between bells and walking her to the next class. Going solo was going to take some getting used to. Especially at lunch, he realized, when he looked around for a place to sit and could not find any of his teammates there yet.

Oh well, he thought. He took a seat at the first empty table he could find, sat down, began to dig into the fish sticks and mashed potatoes.

A minute or so later, he could feel someone looking at him from the table across the aisle, He turned his head to the right, and that is when he saw her.

At first glance, she was gawky and even awkward in appearance, but he could see that knee-jerk reaction was all wrong.

Not gawky, just tall, something revealed by her long legs reaching out from a black denim skirt.

She had short hiking boots on her feet, a t-shirt with a unique image on it, a movie poster of *The Lost Boys*. She had oversized blue hoop earrings, and tattoo of something he could not make out on top of her left hand. But upon closer inspection, it looked like a bat, as in the *Batman* logo. On her right arm she had another tattoo. It was a rose.

She wore librarian-esque glasses and had her flowing dark curly locks pulled back in a way that said she was trying to hide herself. It was as if she wanted to be different and yet not be noticed at the same time.

He wondered how he had not noticed her before. Then it hit him that she did look familiar. Very familiar. But he struggled to remember why. Where had he seen her before? Maybe in one of his classes from last year?

She may not have been traditionally beautiful in the cheerleader Victorian Secret perfection way that Heather was. But she had…something. Something that made her not just pretty. But downright sexy, at least to Rick.

They locked eyes and he found himself intensely attracted to her.

She was sitting at a table with two other people, a plump, nerdy redhead with catlike glasses and a long, lanky kid that Rick immediately nicknamed Stretch in his head. Stretch and the Redhead were egging her on, intensely trying to lead her forward out of her chair, directing her to approach Rick.

The poor girl was beyond nervous. She looked terrified. But she did finally step out of her chair and make her way toward Rick. He stared at her and tried to smile, completely entranced by this interesting gem of a girl.

"Excuse me," she said. "I was wondering if I could ask you about something. I mean if that would be okay."

Her voice was timid and mousy. But her eyes. There was something there. A focus. A passion. A fire. He felt a vibe. A vibe he had have never felt from a girl before.

"Of course," Rick said, trying to calm her nerves. He motioned for her to take the seat across from him.

"I'm Rick by the way," he said, offering his hand.

"Of course," she said. "I know."

"And?" he asked.

"Huh?" she said. "Oh, sorry. I'm Delila."

The name. It seemed to sound melodic when she spoke it. It sung to him.

Seeing her up close, two things struck him. She was quite cute. Striking actually. And he was now absolutely sure he had seen her somewhere before.

"I'm sorry Delila, but you look so familiar," he said. "Where have we met?"

"Met? Who me? Us? Oh never of course. How could we ever meet? I mean you are…you. And I'm…" she stammered. "Actually, the reason I'm here is I write for the school paper and I'm working on a film project for Channel Sixteen."

Now she really had his interest.

"Oh really? I love movies. What kind of film?" he asked.

"It's a documentary," she said.

"Oh yeah?" he said. "What's it about?"

"Well…it's about…you actually" she said hesitantly.

Before Rick could answer, a stampede of his teammates thundered onto the scene, taking their seats while engaged in the kind of loud, boisterous, testosterone drenched chatter you would expect among a group of high school football players.

Delilia looked aghast as she bounced out of the chair and scurried away while mumbling something about talking more later.

"But Delila…wait," he called out.

But she was gone. She didn't even return to the table with her two friends but vanished from the cafeteria entirely.

"What's with that freak you were talking to?" Todd Wader quipped.

Wader was an outside linebacker. A nasty football player with the size, speed, and skill to be a D1 celebrity recruit in his own right. Nice to have him on your defense. But too much of a hard ass for Rick to handle being around outside of football.

"She writes for the newspaper," Rick said.

"That's right!" Dwight Dean said.

Charismatic, black, six-feet one, a rock solid two-hundred forty-five pounds, and another big college recruiter favorite, Dwight was the team's center. He had a voice almost as deep as James Earl Jones, was fiercely loyal to Rick, and probably his best friend.

"She writes those movie reviews you like reading?" Dwight said.

"Really?" Rick said.

"Yep, the movie chick," Dwight said. "So what did she want with you?"

"To make a movie actually," Rick said.

"Come on man. You fucking with me?" Dwight said.

"No really," Rick said. "Like a behind the scenes documentary thing for the PBS station."

"Hey, why not. Might be a good recruiting piece," Dwight said.

"Not that you need it," Skeeter said.

Skeeter was a junior flanker speed demon who was emerging as the team's major deep threat.

"Them boys up at Notre Dame are all but creaming their pants for that golden right arm of your bro," Skeeter said. "But now that you're single, you should do the film anyway. I mean, she did look kinda cute."

"I think you took too many hits in that scrimmage last week Skeeter," Wader said. "Like I said. She's a freak. And definitely not your type anyway Strass."

"And what do you know about my type Wader?' Rick shot back.

Wader's eyes lit up as he looked over Rick's shoulder and behind him.

"I know because I'm looking at your type right now," Wader said.

Rick looked back behind him to see Heather and her entourage making their grand entrance.

"That's the past," Rick said.

Then he said he said it again quietly, almost to himself.

That's the past.

"And what's the future my brother?" Dwight asked. "This film and the movie chick?"

"Let's just say, I find it interesting," Rick said.

"The film?" Dwight asked. "Or the girl?

Rick looked away dreamily, thinking of his fascinating but all too brief encounter with Delila.

"Both," he said. "Both."

Chapter 4 – Production

Delila spent the afternoon obsessing over her approach and brief encounter with Rick Strasser.

How ridiculous and lame did I come across?

Did he recognize me from that night in the Grove?

Will he even agree to do the film after the way I panicked and bailed? Oh my God, what a flake I must have looked like?

Will I now become a target of mockery for the football team? Did I just blow years of careful hard work trying to isolate to build up protective barriers?

These thoughts and more raced through her head.

"Hey, actually you looked kind of cool and comfortable with him," Suzy said.

"That is, until the starting lineup of the Colts came charging on to the scene," Spaz added. "Buty hey, he didn't say no. And he'll want the pub, so if you ask me Dee, I think you're in."

Her friends were well meaning. But they were about as adept at the art of social interaction as she was. Which was to say they were social morons.

But maybe they were more spot on in their evaluation than she realized. Because as Delila made her way down the hall to drop off her books before heading down to the newspaper room, there he was, standing right in front of her locker.

It was Rick Strasser

At first, she was nervous, just waiting for the other shoe to drop. Was this some kind of *Carrie* style prank he was leading her into with an army of jocks waiting around the corner to mock her?

But the way he looked at her. The way he smiled at her.

It was warm. It seemed genuine.

It felt real. So very real.

"How did you…?" Delila stammered.

"Find your locker?" he finished her sentence.

"Well, if you're going to make this film about me, the first thing you need to know Delila is that I'm a pretty resourceful guy," he said. "That is, when I am motivated."

It took a moment for Delila to take it all in. To process what was happening because it was so surreal.

"You mean…you'll do it?" she asked.

"You know, I had no idea that was you writing those reviews in the school paper every week," he said. "And of course I'll do it. Like I said, I love movies. And a chance to be in one? Hell yes."

"Wow…so…" Delila said, still trying to get her bearings.

"Well, you can't come to practice, at least not yet until I can clear it with the coaches," he said. "They are pretty paranoid about spies from Ely and everywhere else stealing our plays."

"So, meet me outside the locker room doors after practice, say six-thirty," he added. "Cool?"

"Umm yeah," Delila said. "Cool."

"Hi guys," Rick said, looking over Delila's shoulder.

She peered behind her to see Suzy and Spaz standing there, staring with exalted wonderment, as if Tom Cruise or Kevin Costner or some other silver screen icon had just materialized into the halls of Coral Springs High School.

"Okay then," Rick said as he smiled and left. "See you at six-thirty Delila."

The way he spoke her name, it was as if he could sing it. Which, she knew he actually could. For a brief moment she was reminded of that night at the karaoke bar in Coconut Grove.

After Rick left, the three of them just stood there in from of Delila's locker for a second, unaware that a small crowd of onlookers had gathered, no doubt wondering just why the heck someone like Rick Strasser was talking to her.

"Wow," Suzy said. "That was…unexpected."

"Amazing," Spaz said.

"Surreal," Delila said.

Delila quickly emptied the contents of her knapsack into the locker, gathered her writing supplies, and headed down into the newspaper room.

She had a film to prep for.

With her pad and pen in hand and the metallic Sony Hi-8 video camera case next to her, Delila leaned back against the wall, trying as hard as she could to blend into the concrete as the football players began filing out of the locker room, carrying overstuffed gym bags, with towels slung over still damp post-shower hair.

Of course, Rick was going to be the last one to come out of the locker room, putting her nervousness to the test. Adding to the anxiety, a group of dancers from the band came frolicking by. Delila did her chameleon like best to stand perfectly still as if she could suddenly change color and blend in with the concrete wall behind her.

But the strategy had no chance. One of the girls saw her, stopped in her tracks, and pointed an accusing finger straight at Delila, bringing her to the attention of the other girls.

She heard someone say something to the effect of "what is she doing here?"

Delila felt like someone in an S.E. Hinton novel who had just crossed the tracks into the wrong side of town.

The girls began to circle her like a school of piranhas.

"You get lost freak?" one of them called out.

Delila felt her heart seize up. She knew it, always knew it. The second she stepped outside her lane they would be there, ready to slap her back down.

"Back off Carla."

The words came from Rick Strasser as he walked out the locker room doors.

The girls all stood there, frozen with shock.

Rick walked up to Delila and stood right next to her.

"She's here for me," he said, without hesitation and with so much strength and conviction, Delila got goosebumps.

"Really Rick," Carla said. "Now we all know you must be heartbroken over Heather and all, but this kind of rebound is really beneath you."

"I would think that harassing some girl just standing there minding her own business would be beneath you," he said. "But then again, you've been known to do that sort of thing."

Carla gave Delila a long, dirty look. Then gave Rick one too.

"Go on and have your fun with the freak Rick," Carla quipped. "It's your rep buddy."

The bitchy girl gang leader spun around and pranced away, her followers walking behind her in blind, loyal support.

"Don't pay any attention to them," Rick reassured her. "Come on, let's walk."

"To where?" Delila said. "I can't go too far. I need be around to catch the last activity bus."

"No worries, I got you covered," he said. "I live just up Rock Island, less than a half mile away. We'll talk on the way, and I can give you a ride home from there."

"Yeah…that sounds good," Delila said, still trying to take in all that had happened and was still happening.

The thing that really struck Delila the most about Rick, was the way he never backed down to Carla or tried to correct the record about why Delila was there. Anybody else would have stammered, "Oh no. It's not like that. I mean she's just some reporter wanting to some movie about me."

That's the way most people would have acted. But Rick stood there and owned it. Owned her being there. He never wavered. Delila was not quite sure what it meant. But she was sure of one thing. It felt special.

Leaving the high school campus, walking north along Rock Island Road, Delila noticed how the stadium and field stood out behind them, framed by the high school and the majestic light from slightly deep crayon blue sky creeping toward dusk.

"Hold on one second," she said, keeling down to open the metal case and take out the Sony Hi-8 camera.

She walked back toward the street, knelt, pointed the camera up at a forty-degree angle, and adjusted the focus and zoom.

Rick seemed to instinctively know what she was up to.

"What do you need me to do?" he asked.

"Go back up the sidewalk about ten yards, and then just walk," she said. "Kind of normal, while looking up slightly and gazing ahead, as if you are walking out into the great unknown future that lay ahead."

"Roger that coach," he said.

He took her directions and executed them with precision.

Peering into the eyepiece to frame the shot, she could not help but notice how much the camera liked him. He had rock star charisma to go along with his rocket of a right arm. Delila was beginning to see what all the fuss about him was.

"Ready…*The Quarterback*, scene one, take one," Delila said, instinctively naming her now officially in production film on the spot.

As Rick walked up the sidewalk with the stadium, the school, and the sky looming in the background, she carefully tracked him with her panning camera.

It was a perfect shot. Just to be safe, she did two more takes.

"I'll add voiceover to this shot in editing, from stuff when we do the interviews and then edit shots like these in with footage of a one-on-one studio type sit down. Then, I'll intercut all that with actual game footage I'll get on Friday," she said, surprising herself at how this project was coming together so quick in her mind.

"You know, you're really good at this," Rick said.

"At this?" she asked, with awkward shyness of someone not knowing how to take a complement, because she very rarely received them.

"Yeah, at this. Movie making," he said. "You're a natural. Like a Martha Cooledge or an Amy Heckerling."

"What? You know who they are?" she asked.

"Of course. Like I told you Dee…can I call you that? I noticed your friends do," he said.

"Yeah, sure," Delila said.

"Cool," he said. "But yeah, it's like I told you before Dee. I like movies. And you've really got something. A real talent."

She felt herself blush.

Indeed, now Delila really understood all the hype about Rick Strasser.

She had expected a stereotypical jock with a paper-thin personality spouting banal banter and well-worn jock cliches. But he was the polar opposite.

He was…special.

Chapter 5 – The Interview

"Are you ready?" Delila asked.

"Absolutely," Rick said, sitting back in his chair, looking as relaxed as could be.

She clicked on the tape recorder to add a backup sound source to the Sony Hi-8 which was held in place on her shoulder as she carefully framed the shot.

They were on Rick's back patio. He had invited Delila into his house to meet his parents, two younger sisters, and allow her to get some key footage featuring all of them and of the house. He even showed her his collection of *Batman* comic books and sports trading cards, something that would add a wonderful little touch of backstory.

It was happening so fast and all of it seemed so surreal. His parents even insisted that she stay for dinner which she did.

And now she and Rick were having an official one on one interview for the film.

"So why football, and specifically, why quarterback?" she asked.

"What do mean?" he asked.

"You are a smart kid, an Honor student. You have a lot of interests such as movies, baseball cards and comic books. And music…I noticed the guitar and keyboard up there."

She added that last part quicky, just to make sure she didn't jar his memory about the karaoke bar. Even though Heather was not his girlfriend anymore, that subject was still fraught with peril. Why did she keep this from him? How would he feel about her knowing his secret desire to want to go to Miami? Etc.

She went on with the interview.

"And you're a gifted athlete with case full of trophies back there, so you could play any sport," she said. "So why put all that effort and energy into football, and why quarterback?"

He nodded and she could see him pondering the question.

She saw a faraway look in his eyes. Then, he smiled and spoke.

"You remember last year when *Top Gun* came out and it was a huge hit and all the critics dismissed it as just some shallow junky MTV stylized recruiting piece for the Navy?" he said. "Critics can be so pompous and elitist. No offense."

"Hey, none taken," Delila said. "I actually like *Top Gun* and gave it a solid three-star review."

"How about that," he said. "See, I knew I liked you. Now I am sure of it."

Delila felt herself blushing again. That had been happening a lot lately.

"You passed the test," he said.

"Oh?" she said.

"The *Top Gun* test," he said. "Heather, my ex-girlfriend, just hated that movie. I mean what chick doesn't like staring up at a giant screen filled with Tom Cruise for two hours?"

It just occurred to her that both the camera and the tape recorder had been running the whole time. She quickly shut both off.

"Oh, I'm sorry the that. But I can edit all that out in post-production," she said, more to reassure herself than him.

"No problem. Just the Heather stuff. I don't need that grief," he said. "But you can keep the *Top Gun* stuff in for sure."

She turned both the camera and tape recorder back on and nodded for him to continue.

"At any rate, I see *Top Gun* differently than most," he said. "It's about the pilots and why they do what they do. It's beyond the need for speed tagline. What they do, is something very few people are capable of doing. And most people, even if they had all the physical talents needed; eyesight, eye hand coordination, the reflexes and endurance and cast iron stomach to withstand all those Gs…most, people, even if they had all that, still would never in a million years climb up into one of those cockpits."

He paused for a moment, his eyes becoming alive with a look of wistful passion.

"And the reason they would never do it, is because being a Navy fighter pilot, is really, really dangerous, and really hard," he continued. "Now, obviously being a quarterback is not dangerous, at least not like that. But very few people walking around are capable doing it. And even among those few, even fewer are capable of doing it well. That is because it's hard. So very hard."

"Sorry, that just makes me have to ask the question again," Delila said. "If it's so hard, then why do it?"

He answered slowly, deliberately, his eyes alive with even more passion.

"Because, the hard part…*that* is what makes it so great,"

Delila nodded, then stopped the camera and tape.

The first day of shooting had been a smashing success. She had acquired a ton of good material.

And the subject of her film?

There was a lot more to Rick Strasser than she could have ever imagined.

So much more.

Chapter 6 – The Big Game With Ely

Delila tried venturing out to attend a home football game early on during her sophomore year and it was too much. The crowd packed into the stands like sardines, the religious like furor of the ritualism, and most of all, the people. Lots and lots of people.

It was the ultimate antagonist to someone with a raging case of social anxiety, and at the time, it was devastatingly overwhelming. But now, as she roamed the sidelines to get some establishing shots of the crowd filtering into the stands as the two competing teams went through their warm-ups, it felt so much different. Delila not only felt in control, she was thriving.

Of course, this time out the circumstances were completely different.

It was an away game at Pompano Municipal Stadium near the Deerfield Beach border, so she did not feel like she was facing the entire student body of Coral Springs High. And even though there were swarming crowds everywhere, including a couple vans from local TV stations with a complete camera crew, the chaotic atmosphere helped her remain invisible, even as she clutched the Sony Hi-8 camera to continue getting so many valuable shots.

At this moment, moving about the perimeter of the field, she felt like real director. Tonight was expected to be a standing room only crowd of five thousand plus and as people began to pour into the stands, the atmosphere was already super charged.

The other aspect making this high school football experience so much better that the last was that now she actually understood what the hell was happening. Before, football to her was like a statistics class to someone who hated math. But through her research, talking with Rick, and prepping for the film, she understood that even though this was a non-conference game, it was huge event in the fanatical world of Florida high school football.

Thanks to an accelerating population migration southward into the state from the Northeast and an exploding pool of athletic talent, South Florida was a hotspot for college recruiters across the country. The area was now considered to home to the best high school football in the country, on par with Southern California, East Texas, and Western Pennsylvania.

Today's matchup was a showdown between two local powerhouses in the AAAA division, the largest of the Florida schools. And Rick Strasser was not the only national celebrity recruit people were here to see. Ely had a pair of legendary running backs, Butch Vig, (a.k.a. Mr. Inside), and Vernon Davis (a.k.a. Mr. Outside).

With all that backstory in mind, as she peered through the lens of her camera, Delila was able to allow herself to be absorbed into the moment and get caught up in the adrenaline of the festivities.

Plus, the colors, the crowd, the insanely rabid enthusiasm, the two marching bands, and then the action of the game; it was all so cinematic. Channel sixteen knew what they were doing when they picked this as the subject for her film. It was perfect.

However, perfect was not the way to describe the performance of the Coral Springs Colts. They were in fact, getting their asses kicked.

A mostly pro-Ely crowd went wild as their team's two star running backs ran all over the Colts defense, leading to a 28-7, halftime score. The points for Coral Springs came near the end of the half when Rick threw a fifty-yard bomb down the sidelines where the wide receiver Skeeter caught it in stride as he crossed into the end zone.

Delila was sure to keep her camera active the whole time, making sure she always had a charged battery and a tape with space. She even managed to get uncomfortably close to the team as they filed into the locker room for halftime. Close enough to hear coaches launching angry F-bombs and Rick spewing a few of his own.

The intensity she saw on his face was wicked. She never understood the sports cliché that he or she is "such a fierce competitor".

Now she did.

She spent half time getting filler coverage of the marching band, (including self-indulgent close-ups of Suzy and Spaz), the drill team, cheerleaders, and the dancers. That is when trouble came her way.

When she was panning across the line of dancers, her roving lens caught sight of Carla, the dancer with whom she had the altercation with that day outside the locker room when waiting for Rick.

The head dancer scowled in anger, and after their routine, she ran straight up the cheerleaders, no doubt to give Heather a full report. A moment later Delila saw Carla pointing her way. Both girls gave her an evil stare so intense, she could feel it from twenty yards away.

Delila remembered reading a Time Magazine cover story about Spielberg where the director talked about how as scrawny nerdy adolescent, he had a target all over him. But he beat back the bullies not by force, but by winning them over when he asked them to be in one of 8mm epic movies.

When Delila tried pointing the camera anywhere near Heather or Carla, they shot her the finger along with a dirty look. It seemed the Spielberg strategy was not going to work in this instance.

No matter, Delila thought. She was mentally homed in on this shoot now, in complete director mode. And no one was going to take that away from her. She would get her revenge when the movie was screened, perhaps even on TV, and those two bitches were not in it.

The second half of the football game started, and it was like a completely different game.

As the Colts broke their sideline huddle and galloped out to begin their first offensive possession, Delila was able to maneuver around and zoom in to capture a closeup of Rick as he led his teammates out onto the field.

His hazel eyes were ablaze with the raging fire of single-minded focus. He played like a man possessed, repeatedly leading his team down the field, zipping the football all over the place, in between defenders and into the hands of his receivers with remarkable precision. Spaz would later tell her those throws were “frozen ropes”.

The furious comeback resulted in the game being tied up half-way through the fourth quarter at 28-28. But at the end of the day, the Colts’ defense could not stop the Ely running back tandem when it counted most. Despite Rick’s second half heroics, the Coral Springs Colts lost to Ely 35-28.

Delila was wired after the game. Exhausted yet exhilarated.

She had no idea football cold be so electric, so interesting, and so intense. It had all been so dramatic. And she had captured it all on camera, including the emotional post game reactions of the players and crowd.

After the crowd funneled out, she packed up the Sony Hi-8 and a half dozen full cartridges. It was all coming together she thought. Between the interview with Rick, the coverage of his family and all the game night stuff, all she needed was a good summary narration and some transition footage. The main shoot was over. She was ready to go down to the station’s production studio to access the Avid editor and begin post-production on Monday. She wondered if the school’s musical director Mr. Hawkin’s knew someone who could compose an original score for her to use. Or perhaps he could do it himself if had the time in between teaching class and conducting the marching band.

That would all begin next week. But right now, she has somewhere to go.

This morning at school, Rick had come to her locker and asked her to come to a post-game party at his friend Dwight’s house. She was hesitant, but he insisted.

"You want to give your film a full dimensional view of the subject, right?" he said.

"Well…yes, but…" she said.

"No buts. You must come," he said. "You know, for the film. And…and for me."

The last part, really got to Delila. So she promised to come. But now, after those dirty looks during halftime from the resident queen bitches Heather and Carla, she feared she might be walking into a hornet's nest.

No matter she thought. She had to go. For the film of course.

And for Rick.

Chapter 7 – The Party

Dwight Dean's house was only a few blocks down Rock Island Road from where Delila lived. But that short walk of about a half mile was the most anxious of her teenage years. Had she not given Rick her word that she would be there, she would have bailed out and reversed course in a heartbeat.

But she knew that going to this party was something she had to do. Even her two equally as social awkward as herself friends told her as much.

"Hell yeah you better go Dee," Suzy said. "I mean, he asked you to come. Rick fucking Strasser. He asked you to come."

"You want to be a director? You got the talent girl. But you better get used to dealing with people," Spaz advised, sounding unusually mature.

Yes, she needed to go to this party not just for the film and Rick and because she gave her word, but because deep down she understood she could not hide within herself forever. But as the nervous spasms in her stomach told her, she wanted to stay in that safe zone forever. Because stepping out of it, was just too hard.

But somehow, she fought through the panic and anxiety and made it to the front door as Dwight Dean opened it, motioning for her to enter as the strains of Bananarama's "I Heard a Rumour" played.

"Good to see you here," Dwight said in his silky baritone voice. He seemed sincere and the vibe she was getting from him was that he was an ally.

"Rick's out back," he said, pointing toward the sliding doors at the end of the kitchen.

Delila nodded, said thank you, and began the nerve-wracking walk through the crowd, a crowd of football players and other jocks, student council and homecoming dance committee types, and just popular kids in general, most of them from the nicest sections of Coral Springs. These were people she never in a million years expected to be sharing the same space with. And yet, she thought as the music changed to New Order's "True Faith", here she was, a freak among the elite.

She kept a wary eye out for any sign of her two new diabolical enemies Carla and Heather. So far, the coast was clear.

Despite the presence of some three dozen or so people moving about the family room, kitchen, and the upbeat dance tune, the atmosphere was somewhat subdued. After all, they had lost the game, and that was something this community was not accustomed to.

As Delila tentatively made her way out onto the back patio, she saw him. Rick was standing by the bar and smiling at her as she approached. She drank in the visual. He was a sight for sore eyes.

Rick seemed both surprised and overjoyed to see her. She felt a giddy exuberance bubble up inside her. This made Delila feel wonderful in a way she had never quite ever experienced before.

"I'm so glad you made it Dee," he said, keeping his eyes locked on her in a way that sent a tingle of delight up her spine.

"Can I…?" he pointed toward the bar.

"Sure…a beer would be great," she said.

He poured her one from the keg on ice at the end of the bar. He handed her the cup, then held his up as if to propose a toast.

"What are we drinking to?" she asked.

"To your film of course," he said. "And you winning the top prize in that PBS festival thing. Because anything less than that, then it's like *Gandi* over *E.T*, in '82 and I'm saying the fix is in."

Once again, she continued to be pleasantly surprised by him.

"I'll drink to that for sure," she said as they tapped cups.

She took a long sip of the ice-cold beer and she could feel that there was a moment passing between them. A moment that became interrupted as a slew of Rick's teammates lurked in close behind him, as if they were waiting to be introduced.

And Rick did so, with pride, or at least it felt that way to her.

Each player stepped forward to shake her hand, or at least visually give her a nod along with a "nice to meet you" as a

Depeche Mode synth beat played in the background. One thing for sure, these people. Or at least whomever was in charge of spinning the tunes, had great taste in music.

"So Delila, I heard you are making a film about our guy there," an intense buffed out guy named Todd said. She recognized him as a star linebacker on the team and the defensive captain who went out for the coin toss at the game.

"Now here's the thing…you just make sure you talk to me before turning that movie in," Todd said winking at her. "I'll give you the real scoop."

Todd gave Rick a *gotcha* look.

"Wader, if she puts your mug on camera, that will sink her chances of winning the festival for sure," Rick said.

"Yeah, but it will make the film so much more…interesting," Todd said.

Delila could sense a friendly tension between the two of them. Her brief but intense research into football told her it might have to do with the leader of the defense perhaps not liking how all the attention always went to the leader of the offense. A friendly rivalry she was guessing. But one where they both respected each other.

They were all curious about her, even intrigued. But to a person, very respectful. It made Delila feel good. But it was strange, so different from anything else she had experienced, she was having trouble taking it all in and processing it.

But she had to admit, especially as she saw Rick smile at her from behind the bar, she was having a good time. A really good time.

Then, trouble came walking through the sliding glass doors.

Heather, Carla, and their prancing entourage swarmed out onto the patio, and it was as if all of the oxygen had been sucked out of the atmosphere. Everything went from cool and relaxed, to sour and intense. Even the music shifted, into some nasty piece of screeching second rate metal that totally killed the bouncy club vibe of the place.

Delila felt the breath leave her. The scars of her past came ripping open at the very sight of these stalking, bullying bitches.

She needed to get out of here and fast.

"I really better get going," she told Rick.

She saw Rick's eyes go from her to the Heather/Carla entourage and back to her as she made a quick exit out of the patio, back through the house and out the front door as fast and nonchalantly as she could, thanking Dwight as she flew by.

When she reached the street, she heard Rick call out to her as he galloped out to catch up to her.

"Delila, wait, please," he said. "You don't have to leave on account of them. I just told Heather and Carla that you were here because I invited you and to be cool. Don't let them ruin a good time. Don't give them that satisfaction."

She trusted Rick's sincerity. But had no confidence that Heather or any other others in the clique would abide by his wishes. If anything, they would just be sneaky and even more spiteful. She knew these types of girls all too well.

"No really, I do need to go," she said. "It's been a long night. I'm not used to all this excitement."

She could see the disappointment in his face.

"A long night. But a good one. A really good night," she said.

He smiled.

"I'm glad to hear you say that," he said. "But please, at least, let me walk you home."

"Sure," she said.

They walked together with a nice leisurely stride up the sidewalk of Rock Island Road, side by side, close enough that their bodies were almost touching. Close enough that she felt an urge to hold his hand and was wondering if he felt the same.

"So, we never got a chance to talk about the game," he said. "Despite the bad ending, were you able to get the footage you needed?"

"That and more," she said. "So much more."

"Oh?" he asked.

"What I captured on camera…what I saw was the answer to a question I asked you during our first interview," she said. "The question of why you chose to be a quarterback."

They stopped at the corner of Rock Island and Fifth Court, the cul-de-sac where she lived.

"My house is right here," she said, pointing at it.

"And?" he asked. "The question? What answer did you find?"

She paused for a moment to gather her thoughts. Then she looked up into his eyes.

"The answer is, you do it because the way you play, it is so much more than being a quarterback. So much more than a football game," she said. "What I saw out there on that field was a fierce competitor. A transformative leader capable of inspiring a whole team and an entire stadium. I saw a master conductor in command of a great symphony orchestra. What I saw out their tonight, was a true artist."

He looked at her in a way that gave her goosebumps of delight. She could not help but notice a sliver of moonlight breaking out through the clouds behind him.

And then, he kissed her.

It was a gentle yet urgent and wanting.

So ever wanting.

Standing there on that street corner under the moonlight, when their lips touched and parted, when the soft sensualness of their open mouths joined together, it was warm and wonderful and time itself seemed to stand still as if being manipulated by some off screen special effects guru.

Then, when the kiss ended, they had another moment. But this time no one interrupted them, and Delila was able to savor every last microsecond of the chemistry and magic between them.

"And speaking of artists, true artists, I'm looking at one right now," he said. "Not just with the camera, where you are already looking like the next big indie breakout director, but I'm talking about your writing too. You make reading movie reviews fun and educational and inspiring…and speaking of…"

"Oh?" she asked.

"I saw your summer top ten list in the paper this morning and there are a few things on there I haven't seen yet," he said.

"Like?" she said.

"Well for one, *Dirty Dancing*," he said. "I noticed it's playing down at the Fox Pompano on Sample, and if you don't mind seeing it again…"

"I love to see it again," she said, unable to hide her enthusiasm.

"Good. Then it's a date," he said.

"A date?" she said.

"A date," he said. "Maybe catch the early show at seven tomorrow. Get something to eat after? I can pick you up at six."

Delila had to contain herself. And almost pinch herself to make sure this was real.

"Yeah. That would be…nice," she said.

"Then I'll see you tomorrow at six," he said.

"Yes. And thank you. For inviting me tonight and all that," she said.

"Goodnight," he said, bending down to kiss her again.

"Goodnight," she said after.

Then she dreamily walked up her driveway and floated into her house on a euphoric wave of teenage bliss.

Chapter 8 – At the Movies

The next morning, she called Suzy and Spaz to tell them the news. Then she summoned them to come to her house.

She needed help in putting together a wardrobe ensemble.

She had no earthly idea what to wear or what to do with her hair. They both said they would come by after band practice. She noted how absurd it seemed that the football team had the day off, but the band had practice.

Jeans or a skirt? A button-down blouse or a more in character t-shirt? Boots, flats, or clogs or pumps? Hair up or down? Straight or curly? What kind of lipstick?

Later that afternoon, when they both arrived and the three of them went into her room for a fashion brainstorming session, Delila was relieved to hear that Spaz had already put a lot of thought into it and had specific ideas, and to see Suzy walk in with a makeup case and curling iron in hand.

Suzy pulled out the chair from desk, instructed her to take a seat with a "No worries," she said opening the makeup case while plugging in a curling iron. "I got you covered girl."

Spaz went straight for her closet, carefully shuffling the hangers until he emerged with an outfit that he declared "the shit."

He delicately placed his ensemble of choice out across the bed. It was a short fake leather black skirt, a mustard loose fitting button-up blouse, and a one of her movie-themed t-shirts to wear underneath it. And this particular t-shirt was a rarity and totally appropriate considering the movie they were going to see; the one sheet poster for the 1983 Francis Ford Coppola film, *The Outsiders*, featuring a young Patrick Swayze.

"And for shoes?" Delila asked.

"Your black boots of course," Spaz said. "Now most girls would feel the need to jack up their height with pumps when going out with someone six foot-four. But you're five-nine, the perfect height for him so no need to torture your feet for a few extra inches that you don't need."

"Dude? Damn!" Suzy said. "Remind me to make sure I consult with you if I ever get asked out on a date."

"Well double damn for you girl," Delila said about thirty minutes later, looking in the mirror at her teased-out hair and perfect make-up.

"Really Suzy, I never looked this good in my life," Delila said. "I feel like I'm about to be in a music video directed by Mary Lambert."

"Well, hey, you gave me a lot to work with," Suzy said. "And anybody with a brain, or eyes for that matter, would take you over that bitch cunt Heather or any of her skanky sidekicks."

"Fucking hey," Spaz said. "This is your night, Dee."

"Yes," Suzy said. "So have fun."

"Hey, this is our night. One for the freaks," Delila said. "And I will. I promise."

And Delila did indeed make good on her promise.

The evening started out with that longstanding tradition of Rick coming inside the house to meet her parents while he waited for her to finish getting ready.

From her bedroom she could hear Rick being as charming, warm, and funny as you'd expect while her parents (and little brother Jeff) gushed and swooned over him. And much to her embarrassment, she could hear her dad and Jeff asking for his autograph…several times.

Are you kidding me, she thought.

After applying the final touches to her hair and lips, she stepped into her boots, zipped them up, and walked down the stairs to make her entrance. She was so nervous because she had no idea what to expect. No idea how Rick would think she looked.

She walked down into the living room and the conversation stopped as Rick stood up from the couch and stared. All eyes were upon her. And Rick…the look on his face.

It was a look of shock, in a good way.

It was a look of enchantment and wonder.

It was the look of someone smitten.

It was the look of wanting.

Delila could feel that her entrance was a success. The clothes, the hair, the makeup, the look, it was all working.

The night was off to a wonderful start.

Delila was elated to find out that Rick liked to arrive at a movie early to get "focused."

"Someone's a type A personality," she teased.

"Yeah, and I'm looking at her," he said. "To prove that, I am willing to bet you have a regular place that you always sit. Scratch that. A regular place where you must sit, or else risk being off your game as film reviewer."

He had her down.

"Touche," she said.

"Well?" he prodded. "Where are we sitting?"

"Fourth row, aisle seat," she said.

"I knew it," he said. "We speak the same language."

After they took their seats, the standard THX sound system demo played followed by trailers for *The Pick-Up Artist*, *Best Seller*, *Someone to Watch Over Me*, and two movies she was really looking forwards too, the erotic thriller *Fatal Attraction* and the horror film *Hellraiser* that looked wickedly scary.

When the lights dimmed and the reel changed over for the main feature *Dirty Dancing*, she felt Rick lean in closer to her, and she did the same. It was as if the chemistry between Patrick Swayze and Jennifer Grey was spilling out from the screen and into the fourth row, enveloping the two of them in a warm bath of erotic intimacy, far beyond anything expected from a first date. But this did not feel like any first date. To Delila this felt like *the* date. The date she had been waiting for her whole life.

Afterwards they drove east and ate at the Fridays on Federal Highway, followed by a quick trip to A1A, and then a long walk under the stars along Pompano Beach where Rick made the move, crossing over that relationship milestone of reaching for her hand.

Then they kissed, and for the first time in her life Delila felt as if she were now living in one of those romantic teen movies she usually only wrote about.

Chapter 9 – The Lunchroom Incident

Delila was happy. It really was all working out with her and Rick, because as he had once said, they really did speak the same language.

He came by after practice to eat dinner at her house once a week, giving her parents and Jeff a thrill. Even the family pets, their golden lab mix Sam and their two cats Eve and Billy, were huge Rick Strasser fans.

They talked on the phone nightly, went out every Saturday, seeing movies at different theaters throughout South Florida, ranging from dumps such as the Pompano 4 on Federal Highway, to the spiffy new AMC in Hollywood, to the various bare bones United Artists Theaters peppered all over the area. Together they saw *The Pick-Up Artist*, *Best Seller*, the avant-garde *Slam Dance*, *The Princess Bride*, the exhilarating *Three O'clock High*, John Carpenter's scary and cool *Prince of Darkness*, and the wonderful, endearing *Baby Boom* anchored by a great performance from Diane Keaton.

Delila was in movie heaven, and it felt so good to have someone other than Suzy and Spaz to share that passion with. On top of that, she got to share in Rick's passion as well, as the Coral Springs Colts kept winning, week after week, as Rick continued to dazzle the fans with his arm strength, accuracy, and leadership, while setting new passing records. They won the conference. They even won a rematch in the playoffs against Ely before losing in the state semi-finals to the perennial powerhouse St. Thomas Aquinas of Plantation.

The season had been a smashing success and Rick's stock was as high as ever. Her movie about him was now officially in post-production and really coming together. And her and Rick were getting closer.

Life was good. Real good. Even blissful.

They walked each other to classes, when possible, but agreed to eat lunch separately, he with his teammates, and she with Suzy and

Spaz. That last part really made Delila happy. They could be a couple without losing their individuality. Rick had spent six months being smothered by Heather, so he was just as happy as Delila about this arrangement.

Speaking of Heather, save for the constant dirty looks and evil stares, all had been quiet on the Heather/Carla bullying front.

Delila had mixed feeling about that. She was happy not being harassed. But still, she had this residual feeling of dread in the back of her mind, fearing her enemies were still out there lurking about, scheming, looking for a way to get to her and ruin the teen dream movie life she was now living.

One thing for sure, bullying was far from dead here at Coral Springs High School, as Delila and every else in the lunchroom found out one day.

Rick was the first to arrive at lunch among his teammates, as was often the case due to his schedule of having a study hall right beforehand. The official team table was now at the front of the cafeteria, where he sat with his back to the wall.

The seat offered him a sweeping wide angle full cinemascope view of the place.

He took it all in as he began to eat, but of course, his eyes were drawn over to deep left side of the field (to put in in his quarterback language, the way he visually assessed the space around him due to years of, well, being a quarterback). That is because on the deep left side of the cafeteria was the table where Delila sat. He spotted her back there, smiled and waved, and both she and Suzy did the same.

He wondered where Spaz was. Then a moment later, he saw the gangly awkward teen come out of the kitchen, full tray in hand, making his way toward the back of the cafeteria where Delila and Suzy sat.

Then, once again his natural quarterback instincts kicked in.

He could sense danger, in the same way he could feel the presence of an unaccounted for blitzing linebacker or an impending blind side hit from a charging defensive end. But this time the threat was both more pedestrian, and yet, more complicated to deal with.

The danger was in the form of a mean-spirited bully named Deez and his roughneck group of loud and obnoxious followers.

Deez was from the same neighborhood as Rick and the two had known each other since the first grade. Son of an alcoholic (and said to be wife-beater) father and a distracted beaten down mother, Deez had always been an asshole. He just the kind of kid who went out of his way to be a dickhead. There was even a time, long ago, when he had made neighborhood life a living hell for Rick. But then puberty happened and by the time Rick was thirteen, he was bigger, stronger, and faster than any kid in his or any other neighborhood around.

Of course, nobody ever fucked with him after that. But his newfound power also came with a burden. Because he could not dare to use it, even in the defense of others. Or so he was told.

"Notre Dame won't touch someone with any violence issues. Same goes for any respectable D1 major," his dad said.

"So, if you encounter any situation that looks it might escalate into a fight, you walk away," his dad went on "You hear me Rick? Be smart. I don't care how bad you want to pop someone or how much some loudmouth jerk might really deserve it, you walk the hell away. Because best case scenario, you become a problematic recruit with a blemish on your record with a character issue. And other things could happen. You could get injured. Break your hand throwing a punch. Get arrested. Or worse. So just listen to me when I say this. You smell trouble. Any trouble. Just walk the hell away."

Every coach Rick had played for reiterated the same gospel. You see trouble, you run in the other direction as fast as you can. Once he became a so-called celebrity recruit there were two rules. Stay out of the paper unless it's about your performance on the field. And stay out of the police blotter. That's it. Two rules.

So now, with Rick's quarterback awareness and his spidey sense kicking in as he saw Deez and his goons eyeing up the gawky Spaz as their target, Rick knew he was in a dilemma.

He had power. Power to protect the Spaz's of the world. But should he go against his conditioning? Should he take a risk and use it?

When Deez and his thugs began to sling quarters at Spaz, actual real, hard, metal, dangerous quarters, Rick did not even have to think about it.

He just reacted.

Spaz hit the deck and crouched down into a fetal position to protect himself as his tray and the contents went flying.

Deez and company laughed uproariously, high fiving each other in a sick, twisted celebration of their cruelty. Mob mentality took over as many others in the cafeteria joined in on the jeering spectacle. It was ugly. It was hideous.

He had to do something.

Rick spotted a girl walking out of the kitchen clad in full tennis team garb. She had a racket slung around her shoulder along with a can of tennis balls.

"Can I borrow these?" he said, grabbing the can of balls. He did not wait for an answer.

He held the can in his left hand and took out a ball with his right.

He put Deez in his sights, eyeing up his face as the target.

There was a concrete support beam in the way and people moving around. Rick adjusted his feet and torso, just as he would in the pocket, to get a clear passing lane.

He cocked his right arm back and unleashed the tennis ball with such furious rage, it whistled through the air, zipping in a straight line and at an insane velocity.

A frozen rope.

The tennis ball struck right in the center of the target's forehead with a thudding, violent smack that echoed throughout the cafeteria. It was so loud, everyone froze.

"You like that tough guy?" Rick yelled. "Oh, I'm just getting warmed up."

Rick had fire in his eyes as he marched toward the fallen Deez. Already there was a wicked egg swelling up on his enemy's forehead.

A couple of Deez's stooges moved to try and intercept Rick. He countered by reaching back into the can of tennis balls. The goons flinched, covering up in fear of being at the wrong end of one of Rick's missiles.

"You guys like throwing stuff?" Rick said. "Yeah? Well so do I. Except I throw a lot harder and with a lot more accuracy than any of you assholes."

He looked down at Deez and eyed up the growing lump on his forehead.

"Next time I'll do more permanent damage," Rick said.

The goons, there were three of them of them now, pulled Deez to his feet and formed wall around their leader.

Deez's expression shifted from fear to a sinister glee.

"Yeah Strasser, maybe so big man. But the way I see it, we got you outnumbered four to one," Deez said.

Out of his peripheral vision, Rick could see that the entire cafeteria was watching. He wondered why none of the lunch monitors had interceded. But then when he caught a glimpse of Coach Herman waving them off, he understood. Coach was trusting him to handle this. To hold the line without letting it come to blows.

Deez and his gang began fan out and move in on him. He was in a very familiar role here; the quarterback in the pocket with the pass rush moving in all around him. But there were no passing lanes open because there was not enough space to throw any more tennis balls.

"Four on one," Deez repeated. As if trying to get Rick to stand down and submit.

It might have to come to blows after all. So be it, Rick thought. He was six feet four, two hundred twenty pounds, and an elite athlete. He could handle four on one.

But then, a familiar, booming voice echoed from his left side. It was music to his ears.

"Hey genius. You may want to count again."

It was Dwight Dean and flanking his trusted center and loyal best friend was the rest of the offensive line. Staters and backups. All eleven them, known collectively as the Circle Eleven.

Deez and his goons stood there, frozen with shock, fear, and indecision as everyone in the cafeteria watched and waited, holding their breath.

The defeated leader gave the nod to his gang. They backed down, fearfully slinking away to the nearest exit. Rick kept his glaring eyes lasered in on them the whole time, his escalated adrenaline still throbbing.

The cafeteria returned to its normal cadence and somewhere amid the buzzing noise Rick heard Spaz offer his sincere gratitude with a handshake.

After school, Delila's father came by to give her ride down to Channel 16 to work with the editors there in the Avid room to get her expansive opus down to an acceptable running time while still maintaining the depth she was looking for.

She wanted to capture two things with her film, now officially titled *The Quarterback.* To create an in-depth character study about Rick Strasser and what made him tick. What made him special. Not only as a quarterback, but as a person. And she wanted to tap into the atmosphere and energy that surrounded the intense subculture of South Florida High School football.

But truth be told, despite the first-rate editing suite at her disposal and the urgency of the task at hand, Delila's mind was elsewhere. She could not stop thinking about what had happened in the cafeteria today.

For all their lives, Delila, Suzy, Spaz, and kids of their ilk, had been outcasts. Easy targets for the Deezes of the world. But today, with one tennis ball throw from the rocket right arm of Rick Strasser, all of that changed. With the one throw, Rick had rewritten the rulebook of Coral Springs High School.

It was all so overwhelming. Just too much to process. In a good way, to be sure. But it all seemed so surreal. Because in her seventeen years on this Earth, nobody had ever stuck up for her like that, let alone put themselves on the line for one of her friends.

It made Delila feel all so wonderful. And yet, it scared her. And the thing is, she did not know exactly why. What was she so afraid of? Love? Intimacy? Happiness?

But she could not think of all that stuff now. She had to focus on the task at hand, editing.

Each school was given one hour of instruction and then five hours on the Avid machine. The idea was to keep everyone on a level playing field regarding resources, while pushing each filmmaker to work hard, fast, and efficiently, just like you had to do when under the gun in the real world of film production.

Thanks to Mr. Hawkins contribution, she now had an original score to add to her mix. The combination of his keyboard playing backed by ten instrumentalists from the school orchestra, came across as astonishingly rich and full-bodied.

Adding songs was a nightmare. Even scenes where a radio might be playing a popular song in the background could not be used because to get the clearance to use that song meant money far beyond the film's tiny budget. At least she had built-in source music in the movie in the form the Coral Springs Marching Band. But even that required a clearance from the station's legal department unless it was something in the public domain.

But all in all, as the week of editing progressed, Delila could feel it all coming together. Then, as she watched a rough cut with Miss Allen one day, she realized something.

This movie was going to work.

The Quarterback had far exceeded her expectations.

"You've created a fine film. You took us inside. You told a story about who Rick Strasser really is and what makes him tick. Hell, I think you could win the whole damn thing," Miss Allen said. "I'm so proud of you Dee."

When she turned in the final cut to Channel 16, it felt official. She was now a director.

It felt strange and surreal.

But not nearly as bizarre as what happened next.

Chapter 10 – The Fall Formal

They had just seen *Less Than Zero* at the Fox Pompano and were now in the Bennigan's on Cypress Creek having their post movie meal. Delila was telling Rick how she was going to give the film a mixed review. It was sexy and stylish to be sure with a killer pop song soundtrack highlighted by the Paul Simon penned tune "Hazy Shades of Winter" by the Bangles.

"So all that was great and yeah everyone in it is great eye candy," Delila said. "But it felt choppy and disjointed. Narratively it was messy."

"The point of the book is just how empty, vapid, and pointless their privileged lives are," Rick said. "Tough to translate that into an entertaining movie."

She was always surprised and impressed by his insights. Just another thing about him she would have never guessed in a million years before she knew him.

But despite the all the cool movie talk and fun analysis, she could tell something was on his mind. For the first time since she had got to know him, Rick Strasser seemed nervous.

Finally, after they dusted off a plate of fully loaded potato skins, she called him out on it.

"Okay, timeout," she said. "You're executing the offense, but I'm sensing your head's not in the game. What gives?"

"That obvious?" he said.

She nodded.

"You got me coach," he said. "Really, it's no big deal. I mean, ordinarily it wouldn't be because we've been going out for a couple months now so when big event comes up, like The Fall Formal two weeks from now, I would just assume that we'd be going but…."

"But?" she prodded him to continue.

"But with that super cool rebel, outsider, counter-culture streak you got, and which I love by the way…given all that…" he said. "Well, I wasn't sure how you'd feel about something like that. So,

I guess I'm officially asking. Would you like go to The Fall Formal with me?"

Just the fact that thought it through this so much, just to be that considerate as to her feelings; Delila was giddy with romantic glee. She was swept off her feet.

She took his hand and squeezed it affectionately.

"You had me at super cool," she said.

Two weeks meant she had to move fast.

Her denim skirts, hiking boots, and pop culture themed t-shirts would not cut it at an official formal dance. Although, the dress code was technically "semi-formal", it still required something she did not currently possess. Namely, a really nice dress.

It was a dilemma, and there was only one person who could help her solve it. Aunt Val. The next day she drove down to Miami where Aunt Val took her on a shopping mission, a whirlwind tour through the most revered and hippest clothing stores throughout Coconut Grove.

The day had an epic, momentous flair about it as Delila strolled out of dressing rooms, feeling the eyes on her, not in the usual dismissive way she had always sensed from others, but instead with a gazes of admiration, smitten looks of wonder, and even lust in the best way possible.

She had lived her whole life feeling like she had an invisible role with no speaking dialogue in an angsty fifties melodrama. But now all that had changed. Parading the various outfits for Aunt Val and the curios admiring onlookers, she felt like she was now cast in the starring role, but this time it was a romantic teen comedy with a feel-good vibe.

She felt reborn. She felt like a princess.

At the end of the day, she chose a form-fitting white dress with a high hemline and red trim. The exact opposite color scheme of her day-to-day attire.

"Oh my freaking God!" Aunt Val said. "Wow! That really accents your legs and height and, I mean, wow!"

She felt like more than a princess.

She felt like a queen.

Far from being the jealous siblings most friends would be in this situation, Suzy and Spaz were elated at the news that Delila was going to The Fall Formal, and both gave their thumbs up to the dress.

"We get to live vicariously through you," Suzy said.

A movie in the can and on her resume, going to her first official high school dance with a boyfriend she really cared about and who felt the same way about her, and more people reading her movie reviews than ever; things were not going according to her infamous plans, they were far exceeding them beyond anything she could have imagined before the start of this epic, magical senior year.

Delila always thought about everything in terms of movies, and right now she was jubilant protagonist heading toward the defining event at the end of the third act.

The Fall Formal.

Getting ready for such an event was like mounting a complex military campaign. Thank God she had Suzy, who finally confessed to being a secret reader of Cosmo among things.

"What can I say," she said. "I'm a closet girly girl."

"Lucky for me," Delila said.

With Suzy's guidance, and a little help from mother, Delila was able to get ready on time, and when Jeff came running upstairs to announce that Rick had arrived and was downstairs with everyone else waiting, Delila was prepared to make her grand entrance.

Cue the musical score, she thought. Making her way down the steps, she could almost here the soaring strains of the orchestra, particularly the love theme as Rick smiled at her with loving, wide-eyed wonder, as if he had never before seen such a vision.

It was the most cinematic moment of Delila's life.

She and Rick posed as her parents too multiple pictures, both in the living room and outside near the live oak tree in the front yard.

She had never seen her parents so elated, so proud of her. Even Jeff and the pets were beaming.

So, it was with much fanfare jubilation that Delila and Rick got into his spiffed up metallic blue Dodge Charger and head to the epic event.

The Fall Formal was held at the Weston on Cypress Creek in Fort Lauderdale, a pristine, sprawling hotel that specialized in such events. When they arrived at the hotel and pulled up to the valet, Delila imagined that she was stepping out onto her own personal red-carpet event.

Waking in amid some of Rick's teammates and their dates along with scattering of other hotel guests there for other events, it felt as if there were cameras on her and that this was her big coming out moment. She was the caterpillar who had undergone a magical metamorphosis and was now emerging out of the cocoon and soaring like a butterfly.

It was all so dreamy, so vivid and hyper real, so John Hughs-esque, so teenage movie cliché, and so fantastically romantic and wonderful.

And it stayed that way through the appetizers and dinner, where she engaged in relaxed conversation with Dwight and his girlfriend Stefie, and Skeeter and his date Jade. She felt so at ease, participating in dialogue, and not feeling a trace of the social anxiety that had dogged her since her nightmarish Junior High days.

And it stayed that way through the chill inducing moment when Rick took her hand, leading her to the dance floor for an epically memorable first dance.

She gently swayed to the music, pressing up close against his tightly muscled form, taking in his wonderful smell and reassuring touch, drinking in the sights and sounds and relishing the moment as the romantic strains of Peter Cetera and Amy Grant singing the sentimental ballad "The Next Time I Fall" emanated from the giant speakers around them. If this were a movie, then this tune would be the big MTV marketing tie-in song. It would be their song and this…this would be her big character moment.

Delila really wanted this to be the happy moment. The finale. The final reel. The big, feel-good climax sending the characters off into the sunset as the final credits rolled and movie patrons headed out of the theater in a state of a gleeful, romantic haze.

But later, when she excused herself from the table to make a trip to the restroom, she was hit hard by the sudden intrusion of a harsh reality. That this was not the big happy ending she so desperately craved. This was just the start of the third act, the inciting incident.

After using the restroom, freshening up, touching up her hair and lipstick and doing all the girly girl stuff she had never put a lot of thought into until recently, Delila exited the restroom.

Then, she stopped in her tracks.

She stopped because her path back into the main ballroom was blocked. Standing there before her with glaring smirks of sinister self-satisfaction were Heather, Carla, and at least a half-dozen of their sycophantic followers, their female version of goons and enforcers.

Delila felt her heart stop for a second and then begin pounding up into her throat. Nothing could come out of a confrontation here. She could not let them ruin her big night. She needed to get away from them and fast.

She remembered seeing another way in and out of the ball room around the other side. As the bitch enforcers formed a semi-circle and began to move in on her, Delila knew she had to find a way to escape and use that other entrance to get back into the ball room from the other side.

"You're in the wrong place nerd," Heather said.

"Yeah, you get lost?" one her followers cackled.

"Go the fuck back to where you belong loser," another added.

"And stay the fuck away from Rick," Carla screamed, inches away from Delila.

Hatred and violence hung in the air.

Just as they were closing in in her, she back peddled, turned around, and ran up the hallway toward the lobby to cross over and take the other entrance back into the ballroom.

The other entrance had an under-construction industrial type of area around it, including a scaffold she would have to walk under to get back into the festivities. Evidently, this was an entrance designed for staff. But no one was around, so hopefully she would not get in any trouble using it.

The double metal doors to the ball room were closed, and as she swung them open and stepped back inside the dance, she felt a drowning, avalanche of thudding, sticky, wetness smack down on her from above, in suffocating wave after wave.

It was a wet, nasty, liquid gunk.

It was caked over her eyes so she could not see. It poured down her throat, making her feel like she was drowning.

She choked and coughed, spitting up the nasty liquid, wheezing to catch her breath. She wiped the gunk away from her eyes until she could see what had so violently drenched her.

It was red, like blood.

And even though she knew it was too thick and sticky to be real blood, she knew exactly who did this and where they got the idea from. As vapid and ignorant as the brain-dead Heather worshippers were, evidently one of them must have seen *Carrie.*

Then as she continued to wheeze and cough and struggle to breath and see, she could hear the jeering laughter. The mocking, cruel, insidious evil laughter.

And there they were, standing there, Heather, Carla and the mean girl gang of bitches, high fiving each other, leading the hideous assault of pure, unrelenting, scorched Earth viciousness.

All Delila felt was shock and horror and terror, and all that she could think about doing was getting out of there.

She turned around and ran out of the ballroom. And she kept running up the hallway, through the lobby, and out into the parking lot.

And then, she kept running.

Chapter 11 – The Aftermath

Drenched in a dripping, sticky, toxic soup of red wine, cranberry juice, some kind of grout mix, glue, and God knows what else, Delila bolted across the hotel parking lot, up through the weeds to the interstate ramp, then up to a tiny sliver of space along the Creekside Highway over pass that ran over the top of I-95.

It was a precarious place to be, potentially deadly, as speeding traffic roared only inches away from her. But that danger hardly registered with her. She was in a state of rage and shock, so devastated that she was hardly aware of her chaotic surroundings.

Something had broken inside her, just as it did back during those awful junior high days. But this…this was so much worse. Because she had been living a dream. Building a life. Even falling in love. And now that was all gone. Poisoned.

Those is charge, and maybe even the universe at large was sending her a message.

Go back to where you belong girl.

Her meticulously prepared shimmering dark locks, the girly girl makeup applied with such care and expertise by Suzy, and the dreamy, and quite expensive, heavenly, perfectly fitted dress lovingly provided to her by Aunt Val; all of that was now ruined, utterly destroyed by a senseless act of wanton mean-spirited hatred.

It was all gone now and all she could do was keep running, as if somehow if she ran far enough, she could turn back time like Christopher Reeve in *Superman*, and then she would be back on the dance floor swaying to the strains of Peter Cetera and Amy Grant as she leaned up against Rick.

But there was no going back.

If life was a movie, it certainly was not a feel-good fantasy like *Superman.* It was more like a dour, bleak, hopeless, paranoid, noirish melodrama. One with a really depressing ending.

So despite the traffic and the danger and the nasty, toxic stew dripping all over her, Delila just kept running.

Until a familiar car pulled up alongside her, the metallic blue Dodge Charger

An exasperated, worried sick Rick called out to her desperately.

Somehow, through the shock and the noise and chaos of the roaring traffic, she made it to the car and got inside.

After they pulled out into traffic and headed west and then north back toward Coral Springs, through the reeling fog that was her brain right now, she heard a deeply shaken and furiously raging Rick.

He said he would get her home and would stay with her and help her parents to get her calmed down and cleaned up. He said the Coral Springs Police would be by to take her statement and ask her if she wanted to press charges.

"And you will press charges, right?" Rick said. "They half to be held accountable and we caught them red-handed."

"What?" she asked. "Caught who?"

She could imagine someone as sneakily conniving and manipulative as Heather rolling over or getting caught so easily.

"Deez and his goons," Rick said. "Skeeter spotted them climbing down from the scaffold and trying to escape out though the kitchen. Dwight and Wader ran outside, cut them off, but they got into a car and drove off."

"So they got away," she asked.

"They ain't getting away with anything I promise you Dee," he said. "Dwight and the others will give their statements to the cops back at the hotel and they know where Deez lives. And if the law doesn't take care of them. We will."

But vengeance on Deez, even if it was his hand that dumped the foul goo that wiped put her fairytale night, that was not the least satisfying. Couldn't Rick see what had really happened tonight? Couldn't anyone?

"So you think Deez and those half-with flunkies he rolls with masterminded all this?" she asked.

"Well, that's what the evidence says," he said. "He was there. Ran from the scene of the crime. And after what happened in the lunchroom, he had the motive. Using you to get at me. Typical of a coward like Deez."

As the car came to a stop in her driveway, in addition to being in a state of shock, pissed off, heartbroken, and devastated, now Delilla was annoyed.

"This was not about you," she said. "Well, it was, but not in the wat you think."

"What do you mean?" he said.

"You spent six months with that girl and you still don't see her for what she is," she said. "

"Heather? You think she did this?" he asked. "But why now? And besides, she broke up with me."

"She may not want you. But she doesn't want anyone else to have you either, especially someone like me," she said. "She waited. Probably planned this for weeks."

Rick grew quiet, as if the extant of Heather's evil was a new revelation to him.

"You have no idea what she is capable of, do you? How much hatred she has inside her," Delila said.

"If she did this…if Deez was just a gun for hire, then the cops will get it out of him," he said. "Then she will be accountable."

Delila just shook her head.

"The word of hoodlum gangbanger punk who had a public fight with the victim's boyfriend, against the word of the head cheerleader," she said. "Who do you think the cops are going to believe?"

Rick shrugged his shoulders.

"You just don't get it," she said. "People like Heather, people connected to money and power with the right family and the right connections, they are never held accountable."

They got of the car and Rick walked her to the door.

"Look, if you don't mind, I just want to go in, get out of these clothes, cleanup and go to bed," she said. "And if you come in, my parents will make us rehash everything, and I'm just too exhausted for that."

She saw the disappointment on Rick's face. But really, she just wanted this nightmare night to end.

"Sure. I understand," he said.

He kissed her goodnight, and under a heavy air of hurt, pain, and uncertainty, went to his car and drove away.

Delila went inside, minimized her contact with her parents as best she could with a minimal explanation, took a long scrubbing shower, then went to bed.

But sleep never came. She stayed up all night wondering if maybe stepping out of her shell had been a colossal mistake. She had been bitch slapped back into her place.

Maybe Heather and company were right. Maybe she did need to get back over to her side of the tracks.

When daylight finally arrived, she was wired, stressed out, exhausted, and felt so defeated.

The next day her parents and Jeff went to meet friends of her parents for a brunch at Houston's. Delila had the house to herself and was thankful for the alone time. It gave her the courage to do what she had to do when Rick came over.

Working up the courage to do something that was purely a reaction of straight up fear. The truth was that she what she was about to do was an act of pure cowardice, plain and simple.

"I'm sorry," she told Rick as soon as he stepped into the entranceway of the living room.

"I can't do this anymore," she said.

"This?" he said looking horrified. Truly upset.

"You mean us?" he asked.

She nodded, fighting to hold back the tears.

"Because of last night?" he said.

She nodded again, wanting to elaborate, but afraid if she did, she would break down.

"Delila, you don't mean that," he said. "You just experienced a traumatic event. Not the best time to make major decisions. You're upset."

"Upset? You bet I'm upset," she said. "You don't understand. You don't know what it's like to walk around in a constant state of fear. Just waiting around to see what they will do to you next. I lived like that before. Where we used to live when I was in junior high. And I can never, ever, go through that again."

"Then don't," he said. "Don't let those stupid jealous bitches have that kind of control over you."

"Rick, they will never stop," she said. "She will never stop. As long as I am in your life…as long as I am on the wrong side of the tracks…they will keep coming after me. They will never stop?"

"So what? Then you just quit? Throw in the white flag?" Rick said. "Don't due that Dee. Don't let them win."

"They already won," she said.

Rick just shook his head. She could see how hurt he was. How frustrated. He did not understand what it was like for her. How could he?

"Don't do this Dee," he pleaded. "I've watched you blossom these past two months and it's been such a beautiful thing. Don't go back into hiding."

"Yeah well, I'm not the only one hiding, am I?" she said.

"What does that mean?" he asked.

"Have you told your dad yet about where you really want to go to college?" she said. "Have you told anyone that you want play quarterback for the Miami Hurricanes?"

His face went blank with shock for moment, and then lit up with recognition.

"That was you? At the karaoke bar in the Grove that night? It was so hard to see from the stage with the lights…but oh my God yes! That explains it," he said.

"Yeah, that was me," she said.

"But why keep it under wraps all this time? Why not say something?" he asked.

"I read the papers, and it sure seemed to me that you did not want to be seen there by anyone from Coral Springs," she said. "And can you imagine what Heather would have done to me back then? When you two were actually together?"

"Yeah, but after that? All this time? And you say nothing?" he asked.

She did not have a good answer for that.

"I don't know," she said. "I guess because things were going so good, I didn't want to risk fucking it up."

"But now it's really fucked," she said. "Because it's over."

"But Dee, it doesn't have to be," he said. "It doesn't have to be."

"It does…because I just can't Rick," she said. "I just can't…"

As the tears came, she said the hardest thing she ever had to say to anyone.

"Please…you need to go. You need to go Rick."

Then, she ran upstairs, held her pillow on the bed, and cried herself into a heart broken sleep.

Chapter 12 – Rick

Rick refused to give up on Delila, because what they had together was special and she was special. Special in a way he had never experienced before. Unique in a way that he had never even imagined before.

He tried. God knows he tried. He called, but she would not come to the phone. He stopped by the house and ended up only talking with her parents because she was holed up in her room "too busy writing" to come downstairs. On weekends she would vanish to Miami to stay with her Aunt Val. During the week he tried to track her down between classes, but she was frustratingly elusive.

Delila had become a ghost.

He tried to reach out to her via Spaz and Suzy, but Delila's self-isolation had become so extreme, even they had been cut off. Rick's only contact with her was through her movie reviews each week in the school paper, and even those essays, though as well-written and insightful as ever, had taken on a tinge of aching sadness.

The rest of November was a brutal month, and Thanksgiving was awful. But it was also the time for Rick to finally step up and stop doing what he had accused Delila of, operating out of fear.

After Thanksgiving dinner, he finally had the talk with his parents and told them he was going to sign a letter of intent to attend the University of Miami and play football for the Hurricanes.

It was uncomfortable, to say the least. At first, his dad pushed back hard and refused to accept it. But Rick gave no ground.

"This is my choice Dad," he said. "You had your career. Your time. This…this is mine."

After a few tense days, with the help of his mother's support, his dad finally came around.

Thankfully, the miserable month of November ended and gave way to December. Thankfully because December offered hope through two events.

One, Delila's film *The Quarterback* would be screened on PBS nationwide followed by the announcement of the winner of the festival once all the films were screened.

Two, the school was holding its annual December talent show, and Rick had an idea about something he wanted to do. Something that he hoped he use to reach out and break through to the only thing that had been on his mind day and night.

Delila.

Chapter 13 – Delila

Delila went to classes. She spent weekends at her Aunt Val's, where she would go to the movies by herself at the Coconut Grove AMC.

She would write her reviews for the paper. Most important of all, aside from her Aunt Val and the necessary functional contact with her parents and brother, she avoided all human contact.

She even cut off Suzy and Spaz because she just didn't want to hear about what a big mistake she made breaking up with Rick and that she was letting the bad guys win by caving into their bullying terror tactics. She did not want to hear any of that, because deep down, she knew they were right.

She saw on the news that Rick had finally come clean and announced he was signing with the University of Miami. He had found his courage. But Delila, just could not find hers, because she never wanted to go through another humiliating, soul-crushing experience again like what had happened to her at the dance.

So, she stayed in complete shutdown mode. Until something happened that forced her out of her self-imposed exile from the human race.

The Channel 16 PBS Film Festival.

Watching *The Quarterback* when it was broadcast was a surreal experience, a rollercoaster of mixed emotions.

Seeing her work playing on a screen where she knew thousands of other people would be seeing it was an out of body episode of complete exhilaration. She had a vision for the movie and had fully realized it to the best of her abilities. People seeing this would really be able to really see Rick Strasser for the first time and get an up-close look at South Florida High School football and the fanatical, religious like following it inspired.

But seeing Rick Strasser in the film. and remembering what it was like to be there with him when filming those scenes, that was the downside of the emotional rollercoaster ride.

It was all so painful. As she watched, it hurt so bad, she could hardly breath.

Finally, after ten consecutive nights of screening movies, Channel 16 was ready to announce the winner of the festival, on a live broadcast on a Thursday night. In keeping with her brooding isolation, Delila watched on the portable in her bedroom while her parents and Jeff watched downstairs.

The Quarterback won. Best Film. Best Director. All the major categories. Delila was now officially an "award winning filmmaker".

But once again, she felt a disorienting batch of mixed emotions. It was vindicating. But it was painfully lonely. Because she had cut everyone off, she had no one to celebrate the victory with.

The next day, right after home room, she was summoned to the principal's office. Not because she was in trouble. But because he wanted to congratulate her.

"Oh, you do plan on going to the talent show tomorrow night, right?" he said.

"Well…actually I did not plan on…" she stammered.

"Then change your plans, because you need to be there," he said.

"And…" he added. "You might want to prepare a speech."

He gave her a wink and a nod, then dismissed her.

Her first instinct was to refuse to go.

Then she thought of Martha Coolidge and Amy Heckerling. She thought of Steven Spielberg and Brian De Palma, and Suzanne Seidelman, and Joe Dante, and all the other directors that she idolized, and she knew that she had no choice. She had to go.

She had to break out of her self-made prison and put herself out there.

Chapter 14 – Aunt Val

The day of the talent show Delila received an unexpected and welcome visitor to the house, her Aunt Val.

Delila noted that as with her last trip up to Coral Springs, her aunt was sans Scott, and that during Delila's recent excursions to Miami he had been thankfully scarce. When Val came up to her room to congratulate her on winning the festival and help her pick out an outfit to wear to the talent show, she came clean about Scott.

"He's history," she said. "And yes, I know, another in a long line of losers for good old Aunt Val, as your mother so succinctly just reminded me."

"No Aunt Val. What does she know anyway?" Delila said.

"Well, it's the truth," she said. "But it wasn't always that way."

She took Delila's hand and sat down next to her on the bed.

"Listen sweetie, I'm not one to give preachy advice, because God knows you already get enough of that from your mom and dad," she said. "But there is something I want to say to you."

Delila nodded.

"Somehow, I always end up with the Scotts of the world, and of course, it always ends badly," she said. "But it wasn't always that way Dee. A long time ago, before you were born, and I was in college, I had someone in my life. Someone really special. I mean, we just connected on every level imaginable. It was intense. But at the same time, so relaxed. It was just felt right. So, so right."

Aunt Val paused for a moment. There was a faraway gaze in her eyes and so much emotion on her face. The emotion of nostalgia. The emotion of pain.

"What happened to him?" Delila asked.

"I, in my infinite wisdom, ended it, just as we were about to graduate," Aunt Val said.

"Why?" Delila asked.

"Well, I told myself it was because it was just a college romance and I needed to let go. I told myself that he had great job offer in L.A. that he really should take, and I wanted to stay in Miami. And that even though he wanted to stay in here in Miami to be with me, that I needed to just cut him loose so he could take that job and then we both just move on. I told myself that even though it hurt, this was all for the best. Anyway…that is what I told myself."

She paused again and Delila could see that the emotional pain on Aunt Val's face was growing more and more intense. It was the pain of regret.

"But the truth of the matter is I could feel how close we were getting. How real this thing was between us. And I panicked. It was fear. Fear of commitment. Fear of intimacy…fear of love…" she went on. "The truth of the matter is that your Aunt Val was a coward. Plain and simple. I had something special. Something that a lot of people go their whole lives without ever finding. I had it, and I pissed it all away."

Aunt Val squeezed both of Delila's hands and looked into her eyes pleadingly.

"Don't make the same mistake as me Dee. Don't throw away love for the wrong reasons. Don't let fear make these important decisions in your life. Don't end up with an empty heart full of fading memories and painful regrets," she said. "Now I don't know if this quarterback guy is the one. But I do know that you owe it to yourself to find out."

Aunt Val gave her a hug as they both fought back tears.

"Now…if you can open that closet over there," she said. "So we can get on with picking out what you are going to be wearing tonight when you walk up on that stage to accept your Best Director Oscar."

"Well, it's not an Oscar," Delila said.

"Not yet," Aunt Val said. "But it will be sweetie. One day, it will be."

Chapter 15 – The Talent Show

The good news was that the Best Director presentation from Channel 16 was going to be the first thing up at the talent show. The bad news was that the Best Director presentation was going to be the first thing up.

Her nerves were insane.

Public speaking had never been a strong suite for Delila at any point in her life. And to have to do this now, after the most humiliating, horrific experience of her life. Part of her wanted to just spring up there, snatch the award, mumble a quick "thank you", just motor to the back of the stage, exit out the fire escape doors, and run home and hide.

But Aunt Val's story, and her deep pain of regret, had gotten to Delila. She knew she had to get up there and say something. Something that mattered. Thinking in movie terms as she always did, she knew this was the main character's big chance for redemption. She had to step up and be big enough for the moment. She just had to.

The parking lot was overflowing. People kept pouring into the jam-packed auditorium until it was standing room only. She swore every single soul in Coral Springs was here tonight Along with two TV stations (Channel 16 and Channel 7) and the top 40 FM pop station Y100.

Damn. This really was going to be a big teen movie moment she thought.

Finally, the time came. An intro piece from the school orchestra followed by opening remarks from the president of the PTA, then on to the station rep from Channel 16 who was here to present the Film Festival award for Best Film and Best Director to Delila for *The Quarterback.*

First a brief trailer for *The Quarterback* was shown, much to the pleasure of the enthusiastic crowd who cheered wildly. Seeing that footage again, up on the big screen, really brought Delila back to those scenes. Back to those special moments she had with Rick. Back to when she knew something special and something real was happening between them.

After the trailer finished playing, the projector went silent, the house lights came back on and the woman from Chanel 16, who somehow managed to be elegant and intellectually nerdy at the same time, came up to the dais.

She gave an impassioned speech about the importance of the creative arts in high school and Channel 16's commitment to it. Next, she said some really nice things about the film and about Delila. Then, she asked her to come up on stage to accept the two awards.

For the first time in her life, Delila could hear people cheering for her. It was a loud, heartfelt, sincere, enthusiastic, sustained cheer. And it made all the difference in the world. She was not as nervous now, and she was ready to make that speech.

She walked up to the stage riding the momentum of the cheers, accepted the two trophies shaped like movie cameras from the elegant nerdy Channel 16 woman who smiled at her while saying congratulations. Then, as the applause died down, Delila walked up to the microphone, adjusted it for her height, took a deep breath, and gathered her thoughts.

She was ready for the big moment.

The auditorium was now filled with a perfect, deafening silence. The kind of silence that the phrase "you could hear a pin drop" was created for.

"In the world of film criticism, it is said that for a biopic to be considered a success, the audience must feel like it got to know who the main character really is. That you need to learn something about the subject of the film," she said.

She paused for a moment, looked out at the crowd. She saw her parents and Jeff and Aunt Val. And a couple of rows back, she saw him. She saw Rick.

"Making this film was a real journey, and I learned a lot about Rick Strasser. I learned that he was so much more than just the star quarterback who all the colleges were chasing after. He was intense and focused when it came to football, as expected…"

She paused as the crowd laughed.

"But I also learned that he loved movies and music and knew an insane amount of stuff about both. I learned that he was passionate, funny, and caring," she said. "And I learned that he was special. So very special."

She looked out and saw Rick. They locked eyes.

"But in making this movie, I did not just learn a lot about Rick Strasser. I learned a lot about myself," she said. "I learned, as they say in the business, what I really want to do is direct."

The audience laughed again.

"And I learned that directing is not easy. As a matter of fact, it's hard. Sometimes, really hard," she went on, and looked out at Rick as she kept speaking.

"But someone once told me that the hard part…that…that is what makes it so great."

She let the moment simmer until she felt herself start to become overwhelmed with emotion.

"Thank you," she said. "Thank you so much for being here and for this wonderful honor."

The crowd cheered and Delila ran off stage just as the tears came.

Delila was so emotionally exhausted that she wanted to bail after her speech, but her Aunt Val would not hear it.

"I drove all the way up here to see you and to see a talent show, and dammit I will see this whole show with you sitting right next to me."

Four acts into the show, she wondered if her parents and Aunt Val somehow knew what was happening or if it was just fate that she had stayed for the rest of the show.

A group of musicians took to the stage with Mr. Hawkins seated at the keyboard, flanked by two guitar players and a drummer. One of the guitar players was Suzy. The drummer was Spaz. But the real headline was made, the true plot twist into finale, was when the front person and lead singer took to the microphone at center stage. And the crowd went wild far beyond anything they had done for Delila or anyone else throughout the evening.

Of course, it was so on the nose, Delila thought. But it was the perfect emotional beat. If this were a movie and she were the director, this is exactly how she would have shot the scene.

It was Rick.

He was up there at the microphone, beaming with warmth and charisma, looking very much like he did that night last summer in Miami when he took to the stage at the karaoke bar in the Grove.

Rick spoke as a blue/white spotlight shined on him from above.

"I want to thank Mr. Hawkins for going above and beyond in helping write this song, and for the band you see up here with me, for bringing it to life."

"The song is for someone…someone special. Someone who means the world to me," he peered out at and locked his gaze onto Delila, looking at her in the way he always did. In a way that always made her feel giddy with euphoric warmth and love.

"This is called, The Movie Girl."

Rick looked over to Mr. Hawkins and nodded.

Mr. Hawkins began laying out an inviting, delicate motif on the keyboard with an irresistible melodic hook that was ever so subtly backed up by the guitars. The backbeat by Spaz on the drums established that this was going to be an up-tempo pop ballad in a B major key.

Then, Rick began to sing, and given what she had witnessed last summer in Miami, it was no surprise to Delila that he sung superbly with inspiring and heartfelt sincerity.

That first day back at school
I saw her standing there
Like a summer dream, she haunted me
I had seen her
But couldn't place quite where

Then she came up to me
Sat down right next to me
And I was smitten as I took it all in
Shiny black curls, red lips, long legs
A Batman tat and a Lost Boys t-shirt
I was so in love, I forgot how to flirt
So in love, I forgot how to flirt

Because…

She's the movie girl
She's cinema
She became my love story
She's the movie girl
She's magic
It was a movie
And then it became our love story
It became our love story

Football on Fridays
Movies on Saturdays
Like a John Hughs' production
Directed by a French auteur
It was so romantic
Up on the screen, but so real
So, so, very real

I need her
I want her
She's all I can think about

Because…

She's the movie girl

She's cinema
She became my love story
She's the movie girl
She's magic
It was a movie
And then it became our love story
It became our love story
It became our love story...
It was a movie until...
It became our love story...our love story

As the song ended, Delila felt her heart soar with euphoric bliss in a way that she never thought was possible in real life, outside of the sacred space of the cinema. Then after the show ended, as she filed out of the auditorium with her family and the rest of the audience, Rick was standing out there waiting for her.

It was a movie magic moment. The kind of moment that Delila had dreamed of her whole life.

"I missed you," he said, taking her hand.

"Me too," she said.

"Nice speech," he said.

"Nice song," she said.

"Oh, just wait until we get to hear you perform your song," he said.

"My song? Me perform?" she said.

"Yeah, when we go out next weekend. Down to Coconut Grove. For our reunion at the karaoke bar," he said. "For our redemption."

"Oh really," she said. "And what makes you think I can sing."

"I've heard you singing along to the radio. I got a feel for talent," he said. "And they have the perfect song for you on their play list. One, I just see you singing."

"Is that a fact?" she said. "And what would that song be."

"Take My Breath Away," he said.

They really did speak the same language, Delila thought.

It was the perfect teen movie ending.

www.ingramcontent.com/pod-product-compliance
Lightning Source LLC
LaVergne TN
LVHW052053160826
845678LV00015B/3196

* 9 7 9 8 8 2 0 9 7 6 9 6 4 *